Be Gone

By

Temi Taiwo-Oni

www.temitaiwooni.com

Praise for BeGone

Beautiful, beautiful piece. Definitely, a bestseller. It was difficult to drop, actually. This is impressive; it was a nest of intrigue... and to think it's her first! As in! Well done!

Juwon Odutayo (writer, blogger)

The flow is intriguing. BeGone exceeded my expectations. Its vocab is impressive and its description too.

Niyi Animasaun (The Book Club, Lagos, blogger @tayintayin)

It's a great book.

Francis Gigi (Lawyer, Book enthusiast)

Be Gone is a not so simple story about strength and the will to live.

Temitope Omamegbe, Tajmao (Author, Twice a bride)

Praise for Temi Taiwo-Oni

Temi is an intuitive writer who sees through the human condition.

Eketi Ette (Author, lawyer, Tutor, Brand consultant

Temi is a fantastic writer!
Juwon Odutayo (writer, blogger)

Temi took me through all sorts of emotions until I had a smile on my face at the end. Nicely done

Temitope Omamegbe (Author, Editor, blogger)

BeGone | Temi Taiwo-Oni

BeGone is a work of fiction. Names, characters, places and incidents are either a product of the author's imagination or are used fictitiously. Any resemblance to actual persons, living or dead, business establishments, events or locales is entirely coincidental.

Copyright © 2020 by Temitope Taiwo-Oni

All rights reserved. No part of this publication may be reproduced or transmitted in any form or by any means, electronic or mechanical, including photocopying, recording or any information storage and retrieval system now known or to be invented without permission in writing from the author/publisher, except by a reviewer who wishes to quote brief passages in connection with a review written for inclusion in a newspaper, magazine, broadcast or other media, including digital media and social media platforms.

References of the lyrics to the song "Could you be loved" by Bob Marley and any other lyrics are used in this story under the fair use copyright" laws/provisions.

Cover design
© 2020 MacDonald Iheme
@just_maqdee (Instagram)

Published in Nigeria as an e-book by Temi Taiwo-Oni
www.temitaiwoooni.com

BeGone | Temi Taiwo-Oni

Dedicated to everyone with silent tears, everyone who has set aside their dreams and everyone who wants more out of life.

To my Village

They say it takes a village, and I'm compelled to agree, especially on my journey to writing BeGone.

I can't start this process without saluting the author of my life, the village and all else. I'm eternally grateful to Almighty God, who gifts inspiration, ideas and everything that goes into creating. Thank you, Lord God.

Next come my family, who had to bear with my absence and shortcomings, physically, emotionally, and other ways. Thank you, Taiwo, for your financial support and for bearing with the gaps I created during my journey. Thanks to 'Teniirefunmi, Araloba & 'Nifise for putting up with me, sharing ideas and supporting my writing dreams.

To Ann Ayinde, thanks for being my first fan and reader of my writing since childhood.

To Daddy & Mommy (Yes, I call them that), Sola & Odunola Yusuf and, Adeola, Abimbola & Olanrewaju for supporting me and this book, mainly, especially when I needed it most.

To my mentor, Eketi Edima Ette, for giving me wings and nurturing my confidence in my writing skills.

To my team, Harriet Ogirri (you've always had my back), Temitope Omamegbe (for chiselling, buffing & polishing with me), MacDonald Iheme (for awesome graphics I couldn't afford to pay full price for), Francis Gigi, Dr Monisola Lawal, Bukola Thomas, Morayo Olujobi, Olajumoke Abudu, Oluwatobiloba Ibironke, Kanyinsola Ayodele (for helping me get to the finish line). You're all rock stars and deserve the credit for getting this book out.

To Eberechi Chikezie-Agwara, Juwon Odutayo, Maxwell Omagbemi, Ubong Udoh & Niyi Animasaun, thank you for supporting the vision.

BeGone | Temi Taiwo-Oni

To everyone who has supported my dream to write in their own way, Anthonia Yeside Thomas, Martina Yusuf, Rachael Yusuf, Yetunde Armon, Samuel Armon, Osedebame Okoruwa, Omolola Maja-Okojevoh, Ezinne Alagwu, Tolulope Jaiyeola, Winifred Ehizele, Ade Rahman, Simeon Alfa, Olumide Holloway, Wande Akinpelu, Efua Omoluabi, Elo Omoluabi, Debola Opadiran, Arinola Araba, Tinuola Akande, Abidemi Olaleke, Olumide Akande, Olatokunbo Odulawa, Pat Diaku, Uche Ozor, John Jitan, Adebimpe Ekundare, Adanma Ade-David, Toluwalogo Odutayo, Tonio Okojevoh, Sola Abolude, Othuke Enase, Olawale Olaniyi, Feyisola Abiru, Mrs Ogirri, Wale Sadiku, Jumoke Caxton-Martins, Adetokunbo Sotunde, Idowu Adekunbi & Rhoda Micheal. I'm very grateful to have had your input, and I value your impact.

To my super fans, Atinuke Daodu, Omon Edegbai, Suru Daniels, Ropo Sokunle-Oloyede, Bisi Abidakun, Tolu Baiyewu, Tolu Gbenro, 'Tonia Usidiamen, Rereloluwa Akintola, and all the over one hundred contacts who judiciously followed the preview copy in the last week of May 2020, you all spurred me to turn an old entry I put into the Writivism competition years ago, into a full-blown novel. Thank you! You led this book to its birthing and have charged my inspiration to finish everything else that I'm working on.

To everyone who made an impact, but I have left out. I appreciate your every effort in my journey to this debut.
To everyone whose name should appear in more than one category, you know I love you for being you.

And to everyone new, who is taking a chance on this new writer, I am glad to let you into the world of my writing, and I hope to engage you and connect with you in more ways than one.

Temi Taiwo-Oni

BeGone | Temi Taiwo-Oni

PART 1

As the final blow pounds her right eye, Araba hits the floor hard and fast. Pain surges through her head as the effect of the punch reverberates through her being. She passes out. When she comes to, sometime later, the house is silent. It takes her a while to recollect what happened and why pain is searing through her head. And then, it comes to her.

"Toju! That bast! Arrgh!"

She pouts as if to hiss but stiffens halfway instead, as her right hand bolts to her forehead, where it feels like a pestle is at work. She wills herself to relax, trying to distract herself from the pain. She stays still for a few minutes, then slowly pulls herself to a sitting position, wincing in pain with each movement.
Unable to locate her phone, she drags herself to her feet with tears pouring down her cheeks. With uneven breath and unsteady legs, she slowly makes her way up the stairs and into the bedroom, her sanctuary. The chairs and the wall support her battered frame as she struggles to cover the short distance.

She is a few inches away from her bed when she gratefully slumps on it. Then, she grabs a sachet of paracetamol from the stool beside the bed and tosses two tablets down her throat. Afterwards, she reaches for her water bottle and gulps down the fresh orange juice from breakfast. Spreading out her frame on the bed, she shuts her eyes, takes bursts of deep breaths, and repeats her mantra in whispers.

"Even a bad day is just 24 hours. I can make it through today. I can find strength through the pain. I am more than enough.
Even a bad day is just 24 hours. I can make it through today. I can find strength through the pain. I am more than enough.
Even a bad day is just 24 hours. I can make it through today. I can find strength through the pain. I am more than enough"

As the pain eases off, she drifts off for a bit but becomes aware of a loud ticking nearby. It takes moments for her to turn her head to the bedside clock as she squints to make out the time.

"Almost twelve 'o'clock. The children will soon be back from school," she mouths the thoughts as they come to her. The croaky tone of her voice causes her to twitch in surprise. She grunts to clear her throat.

The thought annoys her because its rude existence ignores the ordeal she has gone through and her state of mind. Her face crumples into a severe frown, and then, as if a piece of glass shattered into numerous pieces in her head, she snaps. Without consideration for personal safety, she hauls her form off the bed and at the wall, willing the wall to crush her. Hot tears stream down her cheeks as she slides back to the floor, howling. At that very moment, Bob Marley's 'Could you be loved' tune fills the air as if from nowhere, interrupting her session of self-pity and torture.

She bites her lower lip at the irony of the words, and yet the appropriateness for the moment is undeniable. It's a ringtone she had picked for her phone because it brought back memories from her childhood and fondness for reggae. Tracking the phone to the dressing table where she had dropped it before her confrontation with Toju, she grabs it and slides her thumb over the screen.

"Hello!"

The call, however, goes off at that exact instant. She immediately dials another number without bothering to check who the caller was. As she waits for the call to connect, she uses the wall mirror to examine the sinister swelling below her right eye. She inhales deeply as the call connects and rings.

"Hello, Chii. Please, I need your help." She pauses to listen, "Please, can you help pick the children from school later and take them to yours?" She continues after another pause, "I'll stop by in the evening to pick them up. Thank you, dear." She twitches, putting a hand to her throat. "Uh! My voice?" She looks around the room, looking for an excuse to give, "It's nothing, just a cold. I'll be okay, thanks for asking."

She quickly cuts the call while still gripping the phone tightly. She trembles at what she has just done. *"That should have been a call for help,"* she thinks to herself, unsure of what she is doing anymore. Slowly, she comes to terms with her unconscious decision to discontinue the farce. She faces the reality that her marriage isn't working and that something has to give, or she will be crushed to oblivion.

Toju!

There is less pain now at the thought of him. Toju has done such a great job of wrecking her, breaking her down one piece at a time, such that there is barely any of her former self left; the real her. The incurable romantic, an energetic, free spirit and sanguine with a horde of friends, is gone. No, that's not her anymore; her essence has been stripped away. The effigy sitting on the bed has no light behind her eyes, just a zombie who drifts through her daily tasks devoid of passion or drive. That is what she has become. Sparkle and Rosie, her twin daughters, are her primary source of momentary joy. It is momentary because it hurts silly that she had brought them into such a harsh life. Little as they are, the twins sense the animosity in the house, and surprisingly, they are well adjusted. They don't cry unnecessarily and are always content to play independently or with each other. They are indeed her pride and sole sources of solace.

The other source, which she has long abandoned, is her passion for drawing. In the early days, she would sit in the spare room doodling away till the dead of the night, pouring images that swirled in her head like the Caribbean calypso. Swirling and swaying, they slid from her mind to the empty sheets, sketching the ideas of her imagination.

Yes, those were the years when her creativity surged relentlessly like a raging ocean. But that part of her life was now tucked away, almost too far from her grasp. Overcome with nostalgia, she hurries to her old wardrobe and rummages through odds and ends of books, jotters, bits of paper, diaries, old photos, and more books. Befuddled, she scratches her temple and gulps down lumps of saliva, wincing as if in pain.

Did Toju find it and dispose of it?

That's something he'd do. He could find yet another way to deprive her of her privacy and starve her of good cheer; do anything to ensure that he solely remains at the core of her life. He has done so much of such over the years that she has become numb to his malign tendencies. If it had been possible to take the twins from her, he would have done so, but there would be no way to explain to the world why his toddlers live apart from him. If there is one thing that he savours more than making her miserable, it's keeping his reputation intact. To the world, he is the doting husband and affectionate father. If only they know the truth.

She grabs her dressing stool, places it beside the in-built cupboard, and climbs on it to reach the duffel bags of clothes. She then starts to drag them down one by one.

Stretching into the farthest corner, she pushes aside the carton of souvenirs that she has piled up over the years, a pair of shoes and her mother's old trinket box, the only heirloom she has. Then she spots it, dog-eared and tattered, but still in one piece, her beloved sketchbook. Sneezing from the dust, she hugs it closely with trembling hands and slowly slides down to sit on the stool. Her lips part, and she silently mouths the words "thank you" and makes the sign of the cross.

Minutes later, she throws some clothes and other items into her Kate Spade polka dot travel bag and goes into the bathroom for a bath. When Araba re-emerges, her face is pale, but the swelling has slightly reduced. She picks up her make-up bag and gets to work. Soon, she looks like nothing has happened. This is one thing she has learnt in this marriage, the *efizzy* of make-up.

After the first few years, she learnt the trick of looking the part and masking her pain. She has gotten so good at it that none of their associates has any inkling of her private throes. The cute, quiet wife, adored by her husband, is all she is in the eyes of the world. Sometimes, she even fools herself that the heartache and battering are just nightmares emerging within the boundaries of her home, alone. She has class and respect, and Toju showers her with affection when she is out there. But, in here, in this haunted house, except for her babies, she has nothing but grief, misery, and pain.

Adorning her face with a smirk to complete her look, she grabs her packed bag and sketchbook and then heads for the front door. She pauses by the picture bracket at the lounge and looks lovingly at her twins. The collage of pictures from their first year always makes her heart tug. She would miss them, but she has to go. Her survival demands that she seek her kismet elsewhere. She takes down the bracket and unhooks two of the frames, placing them inside the small side of her bag.

There is an SUV parked just by the entrance when she steps outside. The driver looks inquiringly at Araba through the open window. She slams the gate securely behind her and checks her phone. She then surveys the vehicle and the bearded man behind the wheels. Pulling her luggage along the brick footpath of the entrance, she cranes her neck towards the front of the car to check the car plates.

"Are you Martin?"

"Yes, Madam. You ordered an Uber?"

Araba nods, gesturing towards her bag even as she appraises his black Benz M class. She is vaguely amused by the irony, driving off in style from the 'house of horror' a final time. Her appetite for the fine things in life had not diminished as her life with Toju gave her the privilege of nice things. Her smile radiates to her eyes while an inner sense of delight takes her over.

The driver alights from the car, collects her bag and places it into the car's boot while she takes a final look at the house. The smile is still tapered to her face, reminiscent of the eye that one gives slow-melting ice cream on a hot, sunny day. She takes a seat in the 'owner's corner' just as the driver starts the engine.

A few minutes away from the house, an unexpected tension wells within her, and the farther away they get, the more it heightens. Hesitation slowly floods her being. Lightheaded and dizzy, she nudges at the window switch, but the glass is immobile. Alarmed, she starts coughing and gasping. The driver peeks at her through the rear-view mirror and rolls to a halt when he sees her demeanour.

"Madam, Madam, you dey okay so?" He asks.

He leans back and notices that Araba is gesturing towards the window, so he winds down quickly and parks the car by the roadside.

"Which kain wahala be this now?" His supposed whisper is loud enough for her to hear, but her attention is on her discomfort.

Instead, she sticks her head out of the window, as far out as is convenient for her. Slowly, her belligerent coughing stops, and her nerves relax.

"I'm okay now. You can continue. Something went down the wrong way." Araba says as she fakes a cough. She's never had a panic attack before. But she does not want the driver to think of her as a weirdo or a mental case.

"Sorry, take it easy, Madam," the driver says as his apprehension lessens. You say I should continue *abi?*"

She straightens up and snaps back to decency.

"Thank you. Please, continue."

Wary but temporarily appeased, the driver shifts the gear to drive and releases pressure on the brakes.

Amazingly, traffic is light through most of the journey, as if the sun has sent the Lagos bustle into hiding. At 36°C, even the air conditioner struggles to cool the car. It is some minutes past three when they pull up at the MM2 airport.

She dashes out after he parks and quickly slips on a pair of Prada sunglasses. After the incident in the car, she doesn't trust herself to maintain her composure with a straight face. The tints provide a shield for her to retreat behind if the panic attack returns. She collects her bag from Martin, the Uber driver, and asks, "how much do I owe you?"

"Two Thousand four Hundred Naira, Madam."

He stretches his phone towards her, ignoring his screen; she counts fifteen crisp, two-hundred Naira notes and hands them over to him. She walks away, dragging her luggage behind her while he is still counting.

Pursuing her, he retorts, "Madam, you gave me..."

She waves him away and continues walking, knowing that he wants to acknowledge the extra notes.

"Thank you, ma." Beaming gleefully, he returns to his car, slams the door and zooms off.

She walks towards the Air Peace airline counter, ignoring the odd stares thrown at her by passers-by. Nothing will keep her from holding up her façade. She eyes the small queue by the counter, glancing at her watch, unable to determine if to switch to another airline. It is three thirty-five already. She sighs. Her adorable darlings would be with Chii now.

She subdues the urge to call them, holding on to her resolve not to look back. They will have to forgive her for now. She needs to save herself first before she can save anyone else.

If you could stifle the pain and steel yourself all these years, you can do this!

Maintaining a straight face, she mentally counts the people in the queue from the counter back to her front. There is the polished gentleman speaking to the officer at the desk, an elderly couple laughing gleefully as they talk to each other, then the baby-faced young lady fidgeting with her phone and a trio of millennials fiddling with their gadgets. The millennials remind her of undergraduates.

Before her gaze settles on the next person, Bob Marley's tune infuses her ear lobes again, alerting her to a call. She gropes into her bag and retrieves her phone. She wrings her nose in dismay when she realises who it is.

"Angela, Toju's p. a.! That snooty girl. Nah!"
She refuses to answer it.

"Not today! Not ever!"

She doesn't even realise she has muttered the words until she hears her voice. She stuffs the phone back in her bag, careful to place it on vibrate as She doesn't want any unnecessary attention. Some song lyrics float into her head from her memory anyway, and she begins to sing to herself, humming the parts she can't remember.

"We've got la la la la,
So, go to hell if la la la la la.
Right!
Love would never leave us alone..."

She brings her attention back to the queue.
The businessman has bought his ticket and walks past her towards the general lounge. Eyeing his manicured hands as he adjusts his frames, she inhales deeply, catching a whiff of his scent.

Versace Eros.

The scent is unmistakable. Her penchant for exotic and unique scents was how she had met Toju in the first place. She wills herself to resume her countdown even as her bag resumes vibration under her arm. Curiosity overcomes her impulse to ignore it, so she yanks the culprit out of the bag once again.

Aunt Sylvia!

Instinctively, her mouth falls open slightly, and her head jerks back.

"Now, what would Toju's older sister want with me?" Clamping her mouth shut, she again stifles the urge to pick up.

Contact with these people will break the jinx, and all would be lost.

Her inner voice does not back down. She inches forward, filling the new gap in the queue. The elderly couple has now left the line too.

Good! The line is moving. My turn, soon enough.

Minutes later, there's just the short Asian man and his Nigerian companion in front of her. Her phone starts to ring again, and she instinctively checks it. It is her tailor this time, so she picks up.

"Thank goodness... hello... hello Rayo, how are you? My top is ready? Are you sure you got the fitting right this time?" She pauses to listen to the other end.

"Okay, o! I believe you."

A furrow deepens on her forehead when she realises that there is no way she can pick up the dress now. She quickly adds, "I'm going out of town for a few days. I'll call you for pick up when I get back."

She pauses again, shaking her head and motions.

"No, Rayo. I can't send you a full payment o! Haba! I haven't even seen the dress, much less tried it on. Ehen, ehen!"

Araba steps forward as the line eases further.

"I can do that. I'll send you three thousand naira today. I'll balance up when I pick it up, and it fits. Okay then, thanks a lot."

Sighing deeply, she ends the call. These are some of the angles she has not considered yet, but she will attend to them tonight when she is safely out of reach.

"Madam! Ma'am!"

The call of the ticketing attendant whips Araba to the present, and she steps forward to buy her ticket.

BeGone | Temi Taiwo-Oni

Her eyes are trained on her phone as she engages herself with candy crush games during the thirty-minute wait in the lounge. However, the sudden buzz of her phone interrupts her game, causing her to pout. It's Angela calling again. She cuts the call, bars the number immediately, and continues her play.

Bob Marley assaults her eardrums again, triggering a slight growl. Had she switched the ringer back on in error? She has had it with that song today. Love and its associated aches are the least things on her mind right now. Everything seems to be bent on shoving that bastard in her face. Her grumbling is barely audible while she tries to retain her composure.

This time, there's no caller ID. Uneasiness sets in as she nervously tries to figure out the reason for so many calls, especially since she barely gets any calls from unknown numbers. Why hadn't she subscribed to Truecaller like the rest of the world? The tune almost ends before she decides to pick up the call.

"Hello, who am I speaking to, please? Uhm... who is this? Okay, Angela, what do you want? What's the matter? Are the twins...? Oh, my God, the twins."

Her hand shoots to her mouth as dread grips her. She barely notices the sarcasm and impatience that seeps through the airwaves from the other end of the call.

"They are fine! Thank goodness. Toju in the hospital? How? When?"

Gazing at the ticket in her hand and then at the rings on her finger, she listens and tosses the news in her mind.

"I'm coming... Where is he? Okay, I'll meet you at Tearatai as soon as possible. Okay."

Dropping the phone on her lap, she wrings her hands together and cracks her knuckles.
What should she do? Can it be true that the formidable Toju Cole is lying fragile at the hospital?
He has never been ill, even a day since they had gotten married, much less hospitalised. Fellow patrons of the lounge pass furtive glances around her, making her shift uneasily in her seat before she pushes her frames deeper into her face.

She is a jumble of emotions as she considers her options. However, it takes only a few minutes to come to a resolution. Perhaps, it is the urge to see his helpless state that spurs her to haul herself over to the family hospital. Or maybe it is her automated sense of duty that has reset itself or some *jazz* of sorts. The announcer calls her flight as she finds herself heading to her next Uber ride.

Rush hour is at its peak, and she is forced to spend three gruelling hours wrestling with her decision to terminate her escape. It is difficult to shake off the feeling that the perfect opportunity to flee is slipping away. She imagines the night ending with finding an energetic and unharmed Toju waiting for her at the hospital. He's probably figured out her escape plan, which was all part of an orchestrated plan to return her to him.

Another part of her, however, cannot dismiss the possibility that she's genuinely needed for reasons other than being the object of his aggression. That thought convinces her that for so much effort to be made to reach out to her by those she usually keeps away from, something is indeed amiss.

As the Camry she is in arrives at Tearatai hospital premises, she relives the blows she received in the morning and remembers that she has received no proper treatment. Reflexively, her hand darts to the bruise beneath her eye. As she starts walking into the reception, she bumps into Matron Eke, who she has known since her prenatal classes; before the twins arrived.

"Good to see you, Mrs Cole; what brings you here tonight?" She stretches out both hands and grips her in a warm handshake.

"You look pale. Are you alright?"

"I'm okay, matron. It's nothing a few pain killers and a good night's sleep won't cure."

She offers the matron a perfunctory smile. After a few seconds, she realises that the woman in front of her seems not to have any inkling as to why she was in the hospital.

"I am here to see my husband." She says, "What room is he in and who is the doctor I should speak to?"

The frown on the woman's face further confirms Araba's suspicion about Toju's accident being a hoax. Araba tilts her head, purses her lips, and adds, "Is there a problem somewhere? I'm here to see my husband."

Sensing a flutter in her belly, she is awash with dread that Toju has set her up.

"Your husband? I haven't seen him at all. When did he arrive?" The Matron asked.

"I was informed that he is here on admission," Araba responds coolly.

With eyebrows raised in confusion, Matron Eke turns towards the receptionist's desk, rubs her fingers against her jaw, and inclines her head for Araba to follow her.

"Come with me, please. I know that we had an emergency case that went rushed into surgery a few hours ago, but I have been busy with several newborn deliveries today." The Matron's voice still holds some warmth, but with a professional edge to it.

The clipping sound of the deliberate footsteps behind her is the only response she gets before confronting the receptionist.

"Please, may I have the patient's name who went into surgery earlier?" Matron Eke asks.

The young man veers his attention to his screen, quickly cascading the Instagram video he was watching before they arrived. He then punches a few buttons and moves his mouse around before nodding.

"Yes, a Mr Toju Cole was rushed in at two-fifteen and underwent surgery at three-thirty today, ma."

Recoiling in shock, Matron's hands fly to her cheeks as she exclaims, "I didn't know."

She glances at Araba and returns her attention to the receptionist, throwing him a stern look.

"What's his status? Where is he now?"

Her voice is now tense, while her piercing eyes convey a need for discretion.

He gazes back at his screen, doing some more typing. He moves his face closer to the Matron and whispers to her, conscious of the watchful, third pair of curious eyes when he looks up. Matron turns to her abruptly and chokes out, "Please, come with me."

They march over to the ICU section, where a few people are gathered in a circle, talking animatedly. One of them stands out because of her familiar silhouette; it's Angela. Matron Eke halts, trying to figure out where the nurses for the section are. Araba, her companion, continues, though at a much slower pace. She approaches with caution, half expecting them to part and reveal Toju, staring at her from their midst. She maintains a stoic stance, with which she hopes to manage the situation if her fears are confirmed.

"Ma'am!" Angela says, inching towards Araba as a hush settles over the rest of the group. At this point, it hits Araba that her earlier anxiety was not unwarranted. Before she can speak up, Matron interrupts the duo.

"He is in pretty bad shape, but he's stable. The doctor says that he still needs close monitoring and may require further surgery."

"May I see him?" Araba quietly asks.

"Let me confirm from the nurses, please." The Matron excuses herself and returns to the nursing station, leaving the two women.

Angela, who's still smarting from being ignored by the boss's wife all day, brandishes a frown, expecting an apology. Getting none, she turns a few degrees away from Araba in irritation, folding her hands between her elbows. Matron Eke signals in their direction and proceeds down the corridor. As Angela makes to follow, she bumps into a human blockade.

"I think I can handle it from here," says Araba giving Angela a pointed look,

Angela returns a fierce glare but eventually backs away, joining the others.

Satisfied, Araba catches up with Matron Eke, who ushers her into the ICU room assigned to Toju. She enters and sees his helpless form on the bed; the peaceful image bears no hint of his violent tendencies. His head is clean-shaven and dressed in a bandage, while his neck is supported with a cast. She draws closer and trembles as she dares to touch him. His warmth and the visible rise and drop of his chest confirm that life has not departed from him yet.

"The nurse says he's been drifting in and out of consciousness." Matron Eke places her hand on her shoulder. "God be with you both at this time."

She gives Araba a light squeeze and excuses herself.

Alone with her defenceless aggressor, she sits in the visitor's chair, pondering the situation's irony. Barely nine hours ago, she was almost lifeless, at his mercy. Now, he is feeble and helpless, literally at her mercy. She smiles brazenly as her lips widen and her cheeks puff up.

What a weird sense of humour the elements have today?

Confident that she is going nowhere today, she settles deeper into her chair. The tables have turned in her favour, and heaven forbid her to be absent at this time. Bringing out her phone, Mrs Araba Cole dials Chii.

PART 2

BeGone | Temi Taiwo-Oni

Toju curls his lips, and his dead eyes study the crumpled figure before him. A close look at him would show the slight heaving of his nostrils, and one can imagine seeing the steam being emitted from them. His hands are still arched into fists, and his palpitating heart almost bursts out of his chest.

Nauseated by the sight of her inert form, he suppresses the impulse to spew on her, looming over her instead as adrenaline deluges his masculine features. He feels the urge to beat his chest, just as King Kong did after each conquest. He opts to clasp his hands together, right in front of his chest, extending them and causing them to crack, like wrestlers and weight lifters do.

When he walks away, a sense of delight fuels his racing heartbeat, and he heads upstairs for a shower. Curiously, she is still in the same position when he passes by, afterwards, on his way out. He pokes her with his premium leather Belitti shoes, bending for a closer proof of life since she seems unresponsive. His icy determination kills off the alarm bells that attempt to ring in his head. Her body is still warm, and he can sense her heart beating, so he rises, thrusting out his chest and swinging his Armani blazer over his shoulder as he walks away. He slams the front door shut, with a bang, unaware that it has triggered her rousing.

Driving out of his street, he flashes an immaculate set of teeth at the street security guard and hands him a crisp, five hundred Naira note.

"Morin sah!" The slender, bleached skinned, Man-O-War veteran collects the cash and salutes Toju, returning his beam and revealing two broken front teeth.

Toju nods without stopping, yet guzzling the adulation from the guard. That's how he expects to be treated, not the kind of insubordination Araba showers him with within his own house. Who does she think she is, opposing him? She knows pretty well that he does not like being contradicted. He wonders what it would take her to get that into her head.

The traffic gets heated, and he regrets this morning's decision to allow his driver to take the morning off to attend to a family emergency. He should have had the office send a driver to him at home. It is noon, and the sun has risen to its hilt. The late morning traffic is unexpected and unsettles him since he has a meeting to attend with his operations team.
He taps his phone, calls up the keypad and dials number two on speed dial. Shortly, the phone purrs through the car speakers and after two rings, a voice rumbles through the speaker.

"Good afternoon, sir," Angela's silky voice filters through.

As crisply and evenly as he can, Toju barks out an order. "Angela, move the meeting forward; I'm held up in traffic."

He ignores her attempt at fawning over him and abruptly ends the call; simultaneously, he slips the gear to drive and eases his foothold on the brakes. The car lurches forward slowly, filling the void left by the preceding vehicle. All is still within the vehicle, and with time, the movement of vehicles improves, but he diverts his attention to his history with Araba.

"Hmmn!" He sighs, ignoring the blaring horns around him.

Araba the elegant.

That was what he had called her when she had introduced herself on the day they met. Her eyes were radiant like the morning, and her gait balanced like a flamingo walking a tight rope. She had visited his company's exhibition stand at one of the expositions fairs they had featured in just when he made a personal appearance there.

He tries to recall whether it was the Made in Naija fair or the GTbank Fashion show but gives up when he can't remember.

She had enchanted him with her astute knowledge of scents and her ability to distinguish fragrant ingredients of most of the perfumes they had on display on that day. A natural Nose is a rare find in Nigeria, so he quickly got talking with her, offering her a job at his perfumery. Of course, his charming wiles enticed her, making her succumb, and together, they created his most successful perfume scents.

The hours spent together, experimenting and mixing, along with, perhaps, the aromatic effects of the fragrances they meddled with, eventually led them to 'Intimacy'. That's the name of the first and most celebrated perfume they created together. That's also what was sparked between them after so many aeons of working close to each other. When the results of the pre-testing of their final sample arrived, it was much better than they anticipated and to celebrate; they shared a bottle of champagne in his office. And then, they shared more, a hug, a kiss, and it all went wild from there.

Wedding bells fit nicely into their plans. Not too long after their formula was copyrighted, they held a lavish nuptial, coinciding with the launch of *'Intimacy'*, their signature Perfume. Eko Convention Centre swarmed with eminent personalities in Nigeria, particularly those from the Fashion, film and music industries. It was one of the fanciest and hottest social events that year.

They continued working together for about a year after tying the knot until the twins came along. Pregnancy had complicated her strong sense of smell, making it also her Achilles' heel. She developed vehement sneezing, which lasted for several hours after being in contact with scents for more than five minutes. She was forced to stop work several months into her pregnancy, though this was providential because tensions had risen between them.

Araba had taken more interest in the factory's operations, querying how things worked. He hadn't liked it in any way and had told her as much. Things reached a head one day when she infuriated him over a matter.

Remembering how Araba raised her voice at him and challenged him in front of a few of his staff that day reignites how he felt.

Deeply provoked by her impertinence, he almost struck her, but he mellowed, containing his fury, calmly asking the other staff to excuse them. As the last person clipped the door shut, he exploded.

"How dare you oppose me publicly, Araba!"

His fist connected with her left arm, sending her a few meters away from where she previously stood. She had screamed, but the sound had not made it beyond his sound-proof walls.

"How dare you oppose me at all? The gall of you!" His nostrils had flared as his breathing became heavy. His face had contorted to resemble a squashed ball of waste paper. "What kind of insolence is that?"
He seemed to have doubled in height as he towered over her cringing frame while shock and confusion permeated her essence.

"Never, ever in your life, talk to me like that again! Do you understand?"
She nodded her head in quick succession, rubbing her right hand against her sore arm. Tears freely poured out of her eyes, causing her mascara to mix with the brown powder her face was coated with, successfully smudging her appearance that morning.

All he could hear was her sniping voice mirroring that incident whenever she spoke to him afterwards. He lost his attraction for her; the love jinx was broken.

He returns his attention to the traffic ahead of him as his mouth unexpectedly tastes bitter. Grinding his teeth, he reaches for the car's glove compartment and pulls out a pack of Welch's fruit snacks, his preferred palliative for his sweet tooth. Traffic has slowed to a crawl, and his irritation resurfaces when he glances at the clock on the dashboard—eleven twenty-three a.m.

The familiar gentle buzzing against the car's centre console where his phone is resting prompts him to look at the radio monitor.
Akugbe
His driver's name is displayed in block letters on the monitor. Clicking the 'answer call' button on his steering wheel, he blares out irritably, "Where are you, Akugbe?"

"Oga sah, I say make a ask you where you dey as a don finish for here. Make a come office straight or make a meet you for the house?"

"Take a bike from wherever you are and meet me at the Seven-up junction before the U-turn. This traffic is maddening."

"Okay, sah! I dey come with *okada*. E fit reach like twenty minutes, but I go reach, quick, quick."

Toju disconnects the call deftly and lets out a loud breath.

Having adapted to his driver's sub-standard speak, he still finds it unnerving whenever he is upset. Akugbe's excellent driving skills make up for what he lacks in grammatical eloquence in many ways. The driver he had before Akugbe had been an HND holder with a bad attitude and poor driving that had cost him his position after barely three weeks of driving him.

When Akugbe had started with him, he had quickly adjusted to Toju's preferences, habits and schedule and quickly grew to understand his expectations.

Tidy and diligent in carrying out his duties, his sharp attention to detail was admirable and earned him the position of the head driver in the company. The fact that he drove the CEO was just a plus because, irrespective of that, his pedigree as a driver was unparalleled. Other drivers were encouraged to emulate him while he inducted any new driver the company hired.

As Toju approaches his rendezvous, Seven-up junction, his mind wanders back to this morning's incident.

The twins had left for their creche before he had made it to breakfast. He was settling into his seat when Araba arrived with a tray, which she set down to his right,

"Good morning." She had mumbled the words and avoided meeting his eyes.

The grunt he offered her in response was so inaudible that she had not bothered to acknowledge it nor look his way. Focused on her task, she placed the stark white plate right in front of him and the stack of fresh toast next to it on the left. Next, she put the bowls of scrambled eggs and crispy bacon slices behind the empty plate, away from him.

His dull eyes wandered with her hands, with each movement she made. Without another word, she took the tray and returned to the kitchen. Toju shifted his gaze to his phone as a beeping sound shrieked through the silence. It was a reminder. He tapped lightly on his screen, cancelling the alarm as curtly as it had started, while a message filled the screen.

DRIVER ... MORN OFF... FAMILY ISSUES.

He remembered typing those words the evening before when he gave Akugbe his consent.

Frowning, he reached out absently, clasping his right hand as if to pick a glass or cup. At the sense of nothingness, he looked up and gathered his breath for a bellow when Araba re-emerged with the tray, bearing a jug of fresh orange juice, a glass and a tub of butter for his toast. Toju clamped his mouth, swallowing his complaint. However, he did not spare her a dirty look, which he gave with piercing eyes.

Rounding his rumination with that scene, Toju manoeuvres his way to a safe spot at the side of the expressway. He looks at the time again, this time on his watch. It is a quarter to twelve. He clasps his hands together and wrings them, cracking his knuckles again.

About to pick up his phone, he hears a sharp knock against the window and is greeted by the calm yet, friendly face of Akugbe. Toju shuts his eyes briefly and bites his lips, suppressing a smile. He unlocks the door and jerks it open into the waiting hand of Akugbe.

"Sorry, sah! Good aftanu. Thank you, Sah!" Akugbe effuses animatedly while Toju steps out. He rushes to the right back seat and opens the door for Toju, who enters before Akugbe gently closes it. He then darts back to the driver's side and adjusts his seat.

Just before he starts the engine, pandemonium breaks out as people from the nearby bus-stop start screaming and running helter-skelter, then a swift whoosh precedes a loud bang, like an explosion. Unexpectedly, a tipper rams into their car from behind, squashing it and the two men inside into a heap of metal and human flesh.

Cars slow down to catch a glimpse of the tragedy, with some occupants even bringing out their phones to snap pictures or record videos, but none attempts a rescue.

Some men from a nearby carwash approach the accident scene and painstakingly help the truck driver out as a crowd of passers-by gather with watchful eyes and anxious movements. This time, more people and pedestrians produce phones to record the rescue and post it on social media, but no one else joins the rescue efforts. The truck driver emerges unconscious but has no visible injuries apart from a swollen forehead from where he hit it against the wheel. He is laid out on the ground, and efforts are made to revive him.

"Den *don commot* the tipper driver," says one woman with a tray of groundnuts balanced on her head.

"Wait o, na Sentio Industry car be that o!" A man says, pointing at the crushed car. Others join in, with each person volunteering a comment.

"Ehen ehen! Na true, na them logo dey de door so."

"Na wa o! Na so accident dey take happen?"

"I know somebody for dia sef. Make I call am."

"Oya! Call naw, make them come see them people."

"Help me check plate number, d phone *don* dey ring."

The sympathiser holds his phone to his ear and alternates between his lips and ear after the ringing stops. He has it close to his lips like a witch doctor chanting his incantations into a charm when speaking.

"Hello! Hello, Nduka! How work na? See ehen, one of ya company car *don* get accident for dis side o!" He puts the phone to his ear to listen before holding it to his mouth again. "I dey Seven-up side. ...Trailer *don* jam am and person *dey* inside!" He listens again and becomes irritable ... "I say you people car *don jam*. ...wo my credit *don* finish, I *don* do my own."

He then taps his thumb repeatedly and aggressively over the 'end call' button as his mouth twists into a frown.

"I *dey* tell am say motor jam, e *dey* ask me say who *dey* inside. How I go *sabi* that one na? When I no be *winch*!"

Complaining to those around him, he merges with the commotion and turns back to watch the unfolding rescue, folding his arms across his chest and shaking his head as people talk excitedly.

The three men attempting the rescue finally extricate Toju's body from the car through the broken window after about twenty minutes of concerted efforts. As they finally pry him from the vehicle, he suffers further cuts to his skin and groans in pain. The crowd bursts into applause, screeching at the proof of life and his extraction.

A woman is sprinkling water on the truck driver when a Lagos State Traffic Management (LASTMA) officer jogs over to her side. He had been directing traffic further along the road when passers-by had called his attention to the accident. Upon arrival, he immediately radios the state emergency services and takes over first aid activities with the two rescued men.

"Another person still dey in the car. Na the driver of the car." One of the rescuers addresses the LASTMA officer. "Him door don jam and the glass for him side no gree break."

The LASTMA officer looks around, searching for something, and speaks up.

"Look for something strong that you can use to break the windscreen." Noticing a piece of metal close to the errant truck, he points at it, saying, "Try that; it may work."

The rescuer picks up the metal and goes to the front of the rubble with his counterparts. It is almost forty minutes before the last two are out of the wreckage. All attempts to stop cars driving past to help out are in vain, as they all accelerate hastily after seeing the accident. Who can blame them? They are wary of being roped into any drama with the hospitals and law enforcement.

The siren of an ambulance is heard in the distance, and subsequently, a black car arrives at the scene. Four people, including the driver, alight from the vehicle in a hurry and rush towards the survivors and LASTMA officer.

"Good afternoon, sir!" The brawny, dark-complexioned man said, taking charge of the party. He is the Chief security officer of Scentio Industries, Toju's company.

The LASTMA officer puts his arms across his sides, preventing their progress. On the other hand, the rescuers attempt to make the men comfortable.

"Good afternoon. Please, stand back. We are waiting for the ambulance."

"Good afternoon," a slim lady with an average height and bronze skin speaks up, squaring her shoulder at the same level as the stocky CSO.

"I'm Angela Elomor, and that is my boss' car. We need to get him to the hospital." Angela attempts to push away the official's hand, but he holds his ground.

"Madam, take it easy. I can't just let you take anyone away just like that."

"Officer Adelana! You do not understand. That is our CEO, Mr Toju Cole. He needs to be dispatched to his hospital now!"

After reading the name tag on his shoulder, the stocky man makes eye contact with officer Adelana. Angela seizes the opportunity to break away from his restraining hand and bolts to Toju's side.

The tired rescuer by his side steps back to allow her full access to Toju.

Before a commotion breaks out, an ambulance arrives. Three people burst out of the vehicle and proceeded to the victims.

"We came with an ambulance, as you can see," says the CSO to official Adelana. Out of options, the official backs away and lets them tend their targets. They lug Toju onto a stretcher and transfer him into the ambulance. Then, Akugbe is placed in the back seat of the black car they came in after the accompanying nurse has examined him. Angela collects the phone number for Adelana and slips her card and the CSO's to him before she enters the ambulance to follow them to the hospital.

"What about the third man? Won't you carry him?" Adelana asks, gesturing towards the unconscious man.

"You said LASAMBUS is on their way; let them carry him," one of the four Scentio staff says. He then sneers, "Isn't he the cause of the accident?"

Unable to stop them from conveying the two men to the hospital, Adelana backs down and returns to the truck driver's side. The crowd is morose as mixed feelings cause most of them to disperse. The rescuers discuss briefly with LASTMA Adelana and go their way amid light applause from the remainder of the crowd.

After over an hour following the evacuation, only a few people are left at the scene as most of them have had their fill of the drama and returned to their activities. The sprinkling of people remaining look pitifully at the sole body lying under the glaring sun, but their spirits get fired up again when the LASAMBUS vehicle abruptly arrives.

LASTMA Adelana, checking the driver's pulse, raises his hands in the air in relief, grateful not to have him die on his watch. He oversees the transfer to the ambulance and follows the vehicle away from there.

PART 3

BeGone | Temi Taiwo-Oni

The siren wails loudly and makes Toju uncomfortable as he lies down on the stretcher. Each ring of the siren reverberates like a piercing orchestra in his head. Not only that, but the prodding and other activities on his body, as the ambulance also makes its way through the traffic flow on the bumpy Lagos roads, is fast becoming excruciating. His body begins to jerk with spasms, and the medical staff pins him down, grabbing one of the loose straps of the cot to secure him on the bed.

"Oh, God! I forgot to do all the belts." He secures Toju by fastening two more straps but pauses on the last one. "This one has broken sha."

Speaking to no one in particular, after the second belt slackens, he loosens the belt to elongate it and then ties it to the smaller piece.

Angela eyes him, shaking her head in unease. She turns her attention back to Toju, frowning when she notices that he is hyperventilating.

"Can't you do something? He seems to be having trouble breathing."
Her eyes widen, and she reaches out to him; her hands are less than an inch above his forehead.

"Madam, move back small, let him have air."

The man pushes her hand away, placing an oxygen mask over Toju's nose and mouth, before turning on the knob.

Toju senses severe tingling around his body and slowly loses consciousness. Arriving at the hospital shortly afterwards, they are immediately swarmed by several waiting nurses and the hospital security guards. Angela is easily dwarfed into the background, and by the time the other car drives in, Toju is already being wheeled away.

"Oga! Please, come and carry our driver too."

She gestures to the security men in concern. Her colleagues throw open the doors of the car to bring Akugbe out. The driver of the ambulance and one of the guards assist in lifting him unto a stretcher brought out by a nurse. Angela and her colleagues then trail the entourage into the hospital's main reception.

"Is there any family member here?" The buxom nurse faces the group. "Or someone who can..."

"He is my boss... I mean the first man... the other is his driver."

Angela's inarticulateness is uncharacteristic of her, and she shuts her eyes and takes in two deep breaths in quick succession. When she resumes speaking to the attending Nurse, her voice is more controlled and even.

"Good afternoon, Nurse; the victim brought in first is Mr Toju Cole, a registered patient with the hospital, the CEO of Scentio Industries."

Unimpressed by the grandeur with which Angela calls his title, the nurse cocks her head to one side, purses her lips and then nods while she writes on the form.

"Is the other man registered here too?"

"No, but the company will foot his bill too."

"His name, please?"

"Akugbe Itomi!"

"Is he on HMO?"

"Uh…! I think so."
Angela looks back at her colleagues in uncertainty but flips her head back to the nurse, quickly recovering.

"It is irrelevant whether or not he is under HMO. I told you that the company will pay."

"In that case," the nurse looks pointedly at her, "You need to pay a deposit of one hundred thousand for each of them before treatment starts."

She turns to one of her colleagues, "Please, help me get my bag from the car. Quickly!"

She then turns to the CSO, "I think it is best if you and Mr James return to the office immediately. I'll call the HR manager ahead, but I need you to impress on him the urgency at hand. I have tried calling Mrs Cole, but she hasn't picked up my calls. I'll try to call his sister as well."
She collects her bag from the approaching figure and finishes, "Go now!"
Turning back to the nurse, who has n busy typing in the information garnered on the computer, she brandishes her debit card.

"Where do I pay?"

The nurse directs her to the receptionist, who issues her two invoices before pointing her to the cashier. Once the payment is sorted, she is directed to the rows of waiting chairs that take up more than half of the reception and asked to wait for updates. Angela settles into a chair and dials Mr Benton, the company HR manager.

"Hello, Mr Benton... Yes, he... they have been evacuated to the hospital... Teratai... I needed to pay an advance deposit, and I think Mr Cole will require surgery." Her voice thins out with emotion at this point.

"It was so horrible. There was blood everywhere. The car was a wreck…. I can't believe people were so inhumane to post it on social media… You're right, sha; we won't have known on time. Please, make the payment and call the hospital to forestall any more hitches. Thank you. Bye."

She takes a deep breath and tries calling Mrs Cole, but after a few failed tries, she dials Toju's sister, 'Aunt Sylvia', as he calls her, breaking the news to her. After informing her of her inability to reach Mrs Cole, she promises to keep her updated on unfolding events and rings off. She crosses her arms across her chest and intersects her legs, sitting upright.

She purses her lips firmly and stares beyond her horizon. Minutes later, she beckons Edet, the last of her colleagues, who had stayed back with her and taken a seat close by.

"May I make a quick call on your phone?"

Edet is taken aback but quickly recovers and hands her his phone without uttering a protest. Angela takes down a number from her phone with Edet's phone and dials.

"Hello… good afternoon, Mrs Cole. It's Angela. I have been trying to reach you all d…hugely relieved to get through to the elusive woman finally; she informs her about the accident and other details, not observing the slight hint of reticence Araba's voice carries.

The cool chill of the air-conditioner nudges Toju to wakefulness. Shivering, he instinctively stretches his hands, pulling the covering over his body. The thin bed sheet does little to stem the coldness of the atmosphere, but his focus is snatched away by the searing soreness gyrating all over him and his constricted neck.

From the quietness around him, white walls within his line of sight, and the metal stand dangling a bag of drip over his body; he realises that he is in a hospital and tries to remember why this is so.

He vaguely remembers parking at a bus stop, but no other memory turns up. Having evaded any major illness since his bout of typhoid fever while in University, he feels strange lying incapacitated on a hospital bed. His reverie is broken by the appearance of a nurse.

"Oh, Mr Cole, you're awake?"

He tries to speak up but can only muster a groan. "Mmhh! Errh!"

She reaches out to him, saying, "Relax, save your strength. The accident has taken its toll on you. You have had one operation, but the doctor says he can't do the other until your blood pressure is stable."

Toju is confused by her comment as he has always had a steady and healthy heart. He remembers being mocked with the title 'tyrant with no heart' by the office physician during a medical workshop at work because his blood pressure was remarkably normal for a man with his business agility.

He recalls laughing at his audacity and cheekiness to say it aloud. He smiles weakly at the memory of that day. The nurse notices his smile and flashes one back in response.

"It is good that you can smile through this, a definite sign that you are a fighter."

When she is done checking his pulse, she briefs him.

"You can't have visitors yet, but the doctor will be back to check in on you. Try to keep your neck still and your body aligned. Nurse Sade and I will be outside in case you need anything. Just press this big button, and someone will come."
She places the call button attached to his bed in his hand and leaves quietly.
Absorbing the information that she had shared, he resigns himself to his predicament and turns his thoughts to processing how he got here in the first place. The image of his wife strays into his thoughts and lingers.

Araba.

He draws out his gnawing memories, wondering if she is waiting outside at the reception. He visualises a crumpled figure on the floor of a familiar room, but the image is blurred. Nevertheless, he tries to reach out, but it floats away, beyond his mental reach.

His mind grapples at the memory of his image walking away from the limp figure. Pain suddenly sears through his head, and he gasps out loud enough to be heard only within the hollow room. Tingling sensations accompany mild pain, dispersing all over his body.

Another image emerges in his mind, and he sees another figure, a man this time, sprawled on the floor by the road, helpless, as a crowd flocks in the vicinity. He looks away from the man and up at the crowd, who are looking down, shaking their heads in pity at him.
At him?

The pain is now fully present, and, unable to bear it any longer, he blanks out after using his last strength to push the call button, which later lies limply in his hand.

A beeping sound floods the room, and a few minutes later, the nurses burst in and begin to fiddle with him.

BeGone | Temi Taiwo-Oni

Sitting calmly in the same chair as before, Araba is relaxed, smiling to herself, reminiscing. Her chat with Chii and the twins a little while ago had been full of mirth.

"Mami, where are you? I dwa a picture of you today.
"Spakul, le me tuk. Mami, when are you coming?"
"Rosie," Chii said, "You can both talk to mommy; let me put it on speaker for you."

The duo had chattered for about six minutes before becoming distracted by a cartoon, abandoning the phone. After that, she had explained to Chii, as briefly as she could, about Toju's accident, begging her to keep the kids for the night.

"I was going to offer to keep them if you didn't ask, anyway. Please, don't worry, ehen! They'll be okay."

Chii's reassuring words are the first she has heard from anyone today, other than the nagging voice in her head.

"Thank you, Chii; I'm grateful, *ose*."

Flooded with relief at her foresight of packing several outfits daily for the twins, a habit she had adopted since their days in cradle class, she had ended the call at her perkiest since the incident.

BeGone | Temi Taiwo-Oni

A sense of apprehension slowly inches into her subconscious, but she loosens up, sure that things are under control now. Now worn out by the day's travails, she slowly eases into a nap, snuggling against the plush cushion seat.

A soft grating sound nudges her from her slumber, and she stirs to a white figure approaching from the doorway. Startled, she shivers momentarily before adjusting to her surroundings and recognising the person.

"I just stopped by to check on you before leaving, m... "

Realising what has just happened, Matron touches Araba's arm. "I'm so sorry I frightened you. I didn't expect you to ha..."

"It's okay, matron. I have had a stressful day; I was on my way to the airport when I got the call. I had to turn back."

"Ehen, ehen! I thought so. It is not normal to come to the hospital with a travelling bag; after all, you're not having a baby, ke."

The matron laughs lightly, causing Araba to nod her head in comprehension before looking furtively at the polka dot bag.

"It's okay. Did your husband wake up at all?"
"No, not yet, matron. He is still asleep." They both turn their attention to the sleeping man briefly.

"Okay then, take care of the two of you. I will see you tomorrow morning." Matron Eke extends her hand to Araba again, this time in reassurance.

"By the grace of God, your husband will be alright, eh. You, too, try and rest. You need strength."
Her eyes seem to say more than her words, so Araba peers into them, studying them in quest of a deeper meaning to Matron's words, but Matron begins her retreat at the exact time. Blinking, the moment is lost.

"Okay, bye," Matron says as she shuts the door behind her. Araba continues to stare at the closed door for a few moments, wondering if Matron was trying to pass a message to her.

A cold sensation grazes her skin hairs stand at akimbo on goose pimples that emerge. She turns slowly towards the bed to see Toju reaching out to her with one hand while the drip tube attached to it dangles in unison.

Edging closer to his innocuous form on the bed, she looks at his face; his brown pupils are fixated on her.

"Toju!"
His name rolls off her lips gently. He trains his eyes on her, almost tenderly. Shutting her eyes, she envisions the swing of his hand before it connected with her face in the morning and immediately flinches, staggering back as if he has just hit her again. She sinks as far back as possible into her seat as fear assails her.

BeGone | Temi Taiwo-Oni

Her heart pulses heavily like a carpenter's hammer on a busy day, and it takes a while for her to remember that he cannot harm her, at least not in this state. Regaining her confidence as her heart rate normalises, she sets Toju's hand back on the bed where it should be, then sits up reflectively.

Araba watches as Toju is wheeled to the operating room the following day. The soft neck brace has been removed, and he looks even frailer now, sprawled out on the stretcher. With Angela standing just a few feet behind them, she comports herself, trying to give a slight hint of emotion or plan. Turning to face Angela, she properly takes in her slightly dishevelled appearance and raises a quizzical eyebrow.

"You stayed the night? Thanks, you didn't have to."
Angela meets her eye and replies, "He's my boss, and I'm obliged to him… and you too."

Unspoken words flit between the two women until a passing nurse unintentionally jabs Angela as she rushes past.

"Sorry, madam."

The nurse's plea streams a little louder than the ruckus around them. Jarred out of the moment of sorts they have just shared, Angela rubs her side to repress the pain after shooting a fleeting glance at the nurse.

"The surgery will take a couple of hours, and I'm going home to change and will stop by to check on the twins. You should do the same and get comfortable clothing."

Angela tilts her head and fiddles with her necklace. Her narrowed eyes hide that she sees some sense in Araba's suggestion. Pangs of pain from slouching on her uncomfortable perch on the hospital chair help drive its truth home.

"I'll update the office... management on the situation and straighten out a few things at the office. Mr Akugbe has been moved out of the ICU, and his wife arrived this morning."

"Akugbe is here? I didn't know he was involved... he did not come in yeste..." Araba's brows are raised in mild confusion.

"I'm sure we'll get the full story when they recover."

Marginally slighted at being cut short by Angela, Araba digests the news, making a mental note to look in on him when she gets back. She checks her watch and proceeds towards the exit with pursed lips.

"I have to leave now. Please, excuse me."

Tugging her luggage gingery beside her, she leaves her puzzled companion behind and makes her way to the exit. Once outside, she remembers that she doesn't have a waiting vehicle, so she strolls away from the main entrance to avoid bumping into Angela again. It takes another twenty, plus minutes before she can secure a cab. As she takes her seat inside the black Corolla, she detects that something is wrong when a sense of dread grips her. Biting her lower lip, she reflects on the last couple of hours. It's not too long afterwards when it clicks to her.

BeGone | Temi Taiwo-Oni

"My sketchbook!"

Her cry alarms the driver jolting him, causing him to squash the brakes.
"Madam! Wetin happen now?" He is overtaken by anxiety, darting his gaze back at her.

"I forgot something... sorry... you can go." She grabs her phone, punching and swiping until her face lights up.

"Martin, abi, what's his name?" She mutters while dialling the number onscreen; she waits for it to connect while cracking her knuckles.
"Madam, can I start the trip?" The driver looks back at her from the right corner of his pupils.

She nods and waves her consent to him while trying to maintain focus on her call. She places the call on speaker and puts the phone on her lap.
In the meantime, the cab driver realises that his apprehension is uncalled for, and he continues the trip.

"Hello, Martin! Good afternoon, I'm your passenger from yesterday. The lady you took to the airport. "

"Hello, Madam." Martin's effusiveness is evident in his pitch. "Thank you for yesterday, Madam. Hope you had a safe flight."

BeGone | Temi Taiwo-Oni

"Err! Mr Martin, did you see my sketchbook... I left it in your car yesterday."

"Sketchbook? Madam, I didn't see anything o! I cleaned the car myself this morning."

"Are you certain of that? I brought it with me to your car. Remember, I was holding it when you collected my suitcase."

"Yes, o... ah, madam, I saw it that time. You didn't carry it down?"

"Mr Martin," Terse and controlled, her voice carries through the car, causing the driver to eye her through the rear-view mirror. "I am certain that I did not take it down with me. Can you remember any passenger carrying something like that or someone who came into the back seat with luggage? Maybe they carried it mistakenly."

"Emm... Hmmm... This book you are looking for must be important o!"

Sensing that Martin is fishing for an incentive, Araba speaks up.

"Martin, help me find the book first. I will compensate you. It's irreplaceable."

"Okay, madam. Make I think small... I go call you back."

The speakers clip to silence, and Araba lightly taps her forehead and shuts her eyes tightly.

BeGone | Temi Taiwo-Oni

What kind of mistake is this, now?

Thin wrinkles of skin form three lines across her forehead, and her expression settles into a scowl.

The driver reviews her in the mirror again.

"Madam, shey everything dey alright?" He asks.

She shakes her head and then nods, one after the other, before staring out of the window with withdrawn eyes for the rest of the ride.

When she alights in front of the house that she left less than twenty hours ago, she is calm and reflective. She pays off the driver, unlocks the pedestrian gate and confidently walks into the premises with her luggage.

Letting herself in, she stops at the lounge and makes to open the side of her bag. However, pausing mid-air, she reconsiders her decision to replace the pictures she had taken yesterday and continues striding into the house.

The empty house seems to mock her with each step taken, its coldness fingering her conscience, jeering at her. The slight sense of triumph she felt last night at the hospital is gone, and in its place, a feeble fear bounces back and forth like a pendulum in her mind. Flopping on her bed as soon as she enters her room, she is gripped by an urge to sink into sleep. Shutting her eyes and basking in the comfort of her plush bed, she relaxes, plummeting into repose.

When she flutters into consciousness sometime later, she realises that just twelve minutes have gone by. Feeling energised by the nap, she takes a shower and puts on a black and white pinstripe, A-line skirt and a grey chiffon blouse and leaves, eager to see her darlings. She is armed with a different bag, this time with clothes and other supplies for the twins for the few days they will be at Chii's.

This time, she drives her sleek, black Touareg, Toju's gift to her last Christmas. Despite their apathy, their reputation is something he never jokes about, so she always has the appropriate paraphernalia to keep up his preferred persona.

In twenty short minutes, she arrives at the block of service flats that Chii calls home. The gateman, one luxury Toju had opted not to indulge in, greets her with hesitation but, after a quick call via the intercom in his small cubicle of an office, ushers her to the building's lobby, where she rides a lift upstairs.

Chii is flanked by the twins when she opens the front door to let her in. Sparkle bursts into Araba's waiting arms first, closely followed by Rosie. Her bags slip off her shoulders as she swoops the two girls into her arms and twirls slowly, basking in their embrace.

PART 4

BeGone | Temi Taiwo-Oni

"My babies! My darling babies!" Araba's voice cracks with emotion as she whispers the words to her children.

Chii, tall, black and compact, is smiling as she pulls the door wide open enough for the trio to amble into her living room while she grabs Araba's discarded bags and follows them in.

Collapsing in unison into a heap on the leather couch, the twins babble while their mother listens as ardently as she can under the circumstances. Though unable to make much of their discourse, she is grateful for how her plans changed.

How could I have thought of leaving left these my adorable ones, my darlings, behind?

She deposits a kiss on each girl's forehead.

I must have lost my mind.

"So, what is the status of mister Tee? I hope he is responding well."
Chii's words jolt her back to reality, and compassion seeps between the two women as they make eye contact. Moments pass. Araba slowly snatches her eyes to gaze at the duo in her arms.

"Girls, you can go back to your play now. Mommy and auntie want to talk."

Rosie strides away from her mother's grasp while Sparkle remains immobilised, unmoved by her mother's suggestion.

Caressing her daughter, Araba speaks up. "He's in pretty bad shape. Last night, he went into surgery and has just gone in, for another not too long ago, ... this morning."

A sense of apprehension besieges her, followed by an ounce of guilt. "I need to get back to the hospital shortly. He can be out at any moment."

Reaching out to touch Araba's hand and give her a soft but firm squeeze, Chii maintains her calm mien.

"I saw the video on instablog this morning... he was lying on the floor with two other people..." Chii's voice is calm, and her words are unhurried. "They say the truck driver that caused the accident didn't make it."

"Ayyy!" Araba's palms clasp over her mouth, and she shudders. The reality of how close she had come to becoming a widow, nudges at her senses.

"You have to stay strong and positive, Araba. He survived the accident for a reason." She gently massages Araba's hand again. "Pray for him and be there for him."

"He... Toju... I... hmmm!" Araba bows her head into her palms, rationalising her thoughts, unsure whether to let Chii into the secrets of the torment from Toju. She struggles with the memory of the blow she received from Toju yesterday and that of the same hand dangling over the hospital bed last night.

"To be honest with you, Chii, I have mixed feelings about this whole thing."

"Every marriage has its horrors, but I know no woman wants to be shrouded in black and christened dowager."

"Dowager ke?" Araba's arched brows and pitched voice both betray her feelings. "I'm not an old woman o... no, not yet. Who uses that word sef? It's archaic?"

The smile on Chii's lips elicits a replica on Araba's, and they both burst into laughter.

"Ehen, ehen! That's what I want you to have on your face. Smile, dear. It makes you feel and look better."

"Thank you, Chii. Thank you so much for everything. I hope the girls..."

"Shhhh! Babe, I know you would do the same for me, so please stop making a fuss. Just focus on getting mister Tee back in one piece, and life will return to normal."

Araba's smile stiffens on her lips as Chii's last words echo in her mind.

Life will return to normal. Is normal what I truly want? No way, not that normal! Something has to change if this fluke will work in my favour.

Abruptly, she jerks up and throws a hug at her friend.

Suppressing tears and her mixed emotions, she represses the revelation of her private life.

"I put a couple of clothes and other necessities in the bag I brought for them. Let me know if there's anything you... they need."

"No problem, dear; I'm sure they will be fine."

BeGone | Temi Taiwo-Oni

Araba is just sliding the gear to park at Teratai Hospital's car park when the ringtone breaks the silence in the car. She retrieves it from its place in the cup holder of the car's centre console and reviews the name on the screen.

Aunt Sylvia.

"Gawd, I forgot!" The words fly out in reflex as she slides the green phone icon.

"Hello, Aunt Sylvia," her steady but withdrawn voice, "I'm sorry, I should have called back yesterday."

She presses the speaker button on the screen and puts the phone down beside her.

"Araba, what is going on with Toju? Angela told me that he had an accident; I haven't been able to reach him."

"Ma, he is... he had surgery... surgeries. He is in the hospital."
"You should have called me. Where were you, by the way? We were all trying to reach you yesterday."

I... I was... I didn't know that was why Angela was calling. I was busy."

"Doing what? My brother gives you enough to cover your needs!"

Araba sucks in her breath and shuts her eyes. Willing the call to end, she considers cutting the call, but the knowledge that Aunt Sylvia wouldn't let up restrains her.

"Why couldn't you have been at his side when he needed you most? You Yoruba girls are always jumping around and forming activity. A bini girl would never do such a thing."

"Aunt Sylvia, please, can I... may I call you back? I just got back to the hospital."

"Got back? You mean you left my brother alone in the hospital? What kind of wife are you?"

Araba shuts her eyes and mentally recites her mantra, allowing the woman's voice to continue to drone in the background.

Even a bad day is just 24 hours. I can make it through today. I can find strength through the pain. I am more than enough.

She does not realise that she has tuned out until Aunt Sylvia's voice rises by some decibels.

"Hello! Hello! Are you still there? Araba!"

"Ma! I'm here. I really need to see the doctor now. I'll call to update you later. Bye, bye."

She rushes her words, clicks off the call, and stuffs the phone into her bag. Composing herself, she steps out of the car and proceeds inside.
The waiting hall is teeming with patients, companions, and hospital staff, particularly nurses. She realises that it is immunisation day with the number of crying babies.

"You're back, Mrs Cole." Matron Eke says as she sees Araba walking toward the wards. "The surgery isn't over yet, but they are almost done. I just went by the surgery room."

"Thank you, Matron." Araba takes her outstretched hand and shuts her eyes as Matron's firm grip sends reassuring sensations to her.

"Nurse Eunice, please, can you take Mrs Cole to the waiting area by the surgery room." A petite, young nurse who has just given a baby to its mother turns towards them, smiling before the Matron steers away, going towards the new mothers.

"Good morning, ma'am. Please, follow me."

Her high-pitched voice warms Araba, and she trudges behind her to the waiting area. The walk takes them from the noisy, busy hospital section to the second floor. They part as soon as she is ushered to the seats along the corridor, metres away from the grey double doors leading to where Toju's operation is going on.

Trying not to be stereotyped, she takes the furthest seat from the doors, sitting tilted in the opposite direction from the door. Unfortunately, without much activity around her, she cannot keep her mind off the procedure in the room behind her.

She then remembers that Toju's driver had been involved in the accident and decides to find out where he is. With no nurse or hospital staff in sight, she opts to call Angela. Looking at Angela's name in Roboto fonts on her screen, she second-guesses her decision, but she strikes the green call icon before convincing herself to forget the matter altogether.
Soothed by the ding of the phone ringing through her speaker, she focuses on what she would say when Angela picks.
However, the call rings out, so she dissuades herself from calling back, choosing instead to text.

Hello, Angela. Thanks again for staying on last night.
Please, send me Mr Akugbe's details. I'd like to check on him if he's still here.

Just as she clicks on send, she hears someone bursting out of the doors and looks up to see a lady in white overalls and glasses. Nervously, she stands up and confronts the approaching lady.

"Hh... ho... how did it go? Hh... how is he?" Araba is unable to hide the concern in her voice.

"It's okay, madam, he's alright. You must be Mrs Cole; I'm Doctor Ama. He's going to be alright."

Doctor Ama stops a few feet short of her and makes eye contact. A mild throbbing starts around Araba's temples and circulates her head. Rubbing her head softly, she grimaces.

"Are you alright yourself, madam? I guess you must have been anxious while waiting here."

Araba manages to murmur a response, not trusting herself to speak as Doctor Ama helps her into the seat behind her.

"Mrs Cole, your husband's injuries were pretty serious, but we strongly believe that he is out of the woods, and his physical scars will heal after the two surgeries yesterday and today. He, however, had a few episodes yesterday, according to Doctor Akinjobi, and we will need to watch him for a few days."

"Can I see him now?" Araba manages to say in a low tone.

"Well, you can, though he is still sedated and moved to the adjoining recovery room where he will stay for a few hours under close observation."

She explains that Toju's response and recovery rate will determine how long he will stay at the hospital but will undoubtedly require some physiotherapy.

Araba digests the information as it trickles in, despite the headache that has now inflamed in intensity. She shuts her eyes, taking deep breaths as sudden light-headedness engulfs her.

BeGone | Temi Taiwo-Oni

"Mrs Cole! Mrs Cole!" The doctor's words float past her ears as she glides into a stupor.

BeGone | Temi Taiwo-Oni

Batting her eyes open, Araba realises that she is lying down and tries to figure out where she is. Several people are moving rapidly and talking around her, and she senses her feet being propped and placed on something soft.

"She's awake," an unrecognisable voice says.

"Mrs Cole, can you hear me?" Doctor Ama looks no different from how Araba last saw her, only that the wrinkles of concern on her forehead are more profound and have multiplied.

"Yes, I can. What's happening?" Her confusion ebbs as she sees the familiar face.

"You passed out a few minutes ago. You need to lie down and relax a little."

Someone straps her left arm and fastens it with a band, and a cold metal grazes her skin. Her arm tightens slowly as air is pumped into the bar around her arm. Just when her arm feels most uncomfortable, the pressure eases away.

"Your blood pressure is moderately low, and you will have to lean back for a while. In the meantime, we will carry out a full blood count and a few other tests, just to be sure there's no deeper problem."

"I'm okay. I'm sure it's just the stress of the last few days," Araba says as she runs her free hand through her hair, groaning lightly.

"I think so too, but I'd like to be certain and not guess. Since you're at the hospital anyway, we might as well check."

The doctor's words are disconcerting to Araba, but she is forced to concede with little justification for her protest or even the energy to do so.
Fortunately, the results of the tests are in her favour, and a few hours later, she is discharged and advised to go home while her husband receives the necessary care.

Upon her inquiry before leaving the ward, she is relieved to discover that Akugbe has been discharged and does not require any surgery. Apparently, despite the non-deployment of the airbag, his injuries were not significant enough to leave any permanent damage.

Angela is waiting outside with a few other staff in the now nearly sparse waiting room when a poised Araba walks in. Mildly surprised at first to see the unexpected callers, she ultimately surmises they are there for Toju, not her.
They all take to their feet and incline towards her, with Angela taking the lead as expected.

"Good afternoon, madam; I hope you feel better now." Araba quickly gathers that Angela knows about her little episode and plays it down by murmuring a response. This is swallowed by the booming baritone of one member of the party.

"Mrs Cole!" He puts out his hand politely, introducing himself. "I'm Wonu Maiye, the company general manager. I doubt we have had the pleasure of meeting, and I'm sorry it's under such dire circumstances."

"Good afternoon, Mr Maiye. Thank you and your team for stopping by. Unfortunately, Toju is not allowed to see any visitors until tomorrow. Even I have to go back home now." Her smile is practised, but she holds it steady.

He gestures to one of the men behind him and waves him forward.

"Speaking of going home, Mrs Cole, Scentio has seconded Onoja to drive you, for now." The lanky, dark-skinned middle-aged man he had pointed out steps forward and genuflects.

"Good afternoon, ma."

"That's unnecessary. I can handle my own driving as I have been doing in the past." Araba's sour expression is at par with her protest, but having none of it, Wonu Maiye asserts himself.

"With all due respect, madam, it is not a courtesy, per se. The management has already decided. With our MD hospitalised and fresh from surgery, the company's future sits in your hands. No expense will be spared to see you seamlessly through this period."

Taken aback, she takes a few moments to reflect on his comments, hovering her gaze from one group member to another. It is a course of action that she did not anticipate earlier but can relate to under the circumstances.

"Very well," she says, trying not to sound defeated. "I guess that after the last 48 hours, it is a development that I can deal with."

She makes her way towards the exit and is trailed by the group to her car. Onoja collects the car keys from her while the others extend their goodbyes to her,

"I apologise about the missed call earlier." She sees Angela's lone frame, standing by the car. "I saw the call and text much later. I was already in the hospital and was working on Akugbe's discharge at the time."

Araba detects sincerity in her voice and is unsure whether to trust it.

"I understand his injuries were not too bad."

"Yes, madam. Thank God for that. He has already been discharged. He will take some time off to recuperate at home."

"That's fine then. Your apology is accepted. I'll see you tomorrow then."

Angela nods and steps backwards, letting Onoja glide the car gently away. The ride home is smooth and uneventful, and Araba is almost lulled to sleep by the time that they arrive. After she thanks him as he hands her the keys, he proceeds to clean her car and Toju's other jeep.

Later that evening, after his departure, she wanders into Toju's home bar, and switching on the crystal pendant lights, she surveys the collection of liquor, even though she has not taken a drop in years. The cabinet has scotch, whiskey, brandy, vodka, red wine, and the cabinet. Toju likes to look the part, despite being a light drinker himself.

Grabbing a glass, she is drawn to a bottle of clear pale liquid with the label Thomas Barton Reserve Graves Blanc, 2017, and settles for it. Partly because the cap doesn't have a cork, like most of the other bottles, she figures that it is a much better option to brandy, whisky or vodka. The taste of the grape is more appealing than the sharp taste of the others.

All is quiet around her as she perches on the loveseat in the living room. Ruminating over the episode at the hospital, she knows that she has to devise a strategy, as taking each day as it comes is not sustainable.

Wishing that she could call someone, she regrets allowing Toju to cut her off from her childhood friends. The tangy taste of the tepid drink matches her reflective mood. Bolstering her subdued mood, she considers her options for handling the situation.

BeGone | Temi Taiwo-Oni

Before the night is at its crest, she is more inebriated than she has been in a while, but she has a plan.

PART 5

BeGone | Temi Taiwo-Oni

Two days later, flanking the wheelchair Toju sits on, she bends her lips from a thin line into a weak pensive smile. Angela, Wonu Maiye and a few of Toju's staff are there to witness Toju's discharge, and they now trail the couple to the hospital car park.

A wave of relief resonates over the group as mild euphoria and chatter linger over their boss' discharge.

Buoyed by the mood around him, Toju places his hand over Araba's arm and looks up at her affectionately. She stiffens under his touch to his chagrin, blinking ever so deftly for a millisecond, throwing him off. The light in his eyes is softened and then extinguished; he bites his lower lip, confirming an initial suspicion and struggling to figure out the reason for the air of aloofness he has been sensing since her visit yesterday, his mood drops. It doesn't feel right that his wife is uneasy and distant around him.

Did I upset her in some way before the accident?

With the doctor's promise that his memories may take time to be restored or that they might never fully return, the future is draped with uncertainty. His memories of the early days of their relationship are as fresh as if they happened yesterday. Still, he feels somewhat disconnected from her because she has neither smiled nor shown any form of affection towards him. Shortly afterwards, she gently and covertly tugs free of him while looking straight ahead. Her face bears no hint of what she has just done.

Toju hunches his shoulders, disheartened by her rejection, while Araba furtively observes his atypical reaction.
His usual response would have been to make eyes at her, signalling her to behave in public, while in the same vein, promising to deal with her upon their return home. Giving him a side glance, she wonders at his odd behaviour since her arrival by his side after the accident.

She considers the possibility that he is playing for pity, even as she remembers the doctor mentioning his amnesia, and curls her lips into a smirk. She has difficulty believing that it is not part of a ploy to deceive her and draw her into a trap.

Boy, if only you know what I've got planned for you!

The thought holds her steady as the hospital attendant stations the wheelchair beside the back door of the Touareg, where Onoja is waiting. As Toju is helped into the car by the duo, he abruptly starts hyperventilating, jerking his upper body severely.
"Take me out! I can't sit there!" He cries out, tightening his grip on Onoja, almost numbing his hand.

Everything happens so quickly afterwards. The stir alarms everyone, and they all gather close by, poking their heads in an attempt to understand what is going on. Onoja and the attendant swiftly move him back into the wheelchair as Toju breaks into spasms.

On her part, Araba instinctively moves closer to him, confused, suspicious and scared all at once. Then, her wits kick in, and she presumes that it is all part of his new act of garnering pity, an act Araba is resolute about not falling for. She feigns continued concern so as not to rouse querying eyes from Toju's fans.

"Are you alright, sir?" Angela's voice weighs heavy with disquiet and prompts a sharp look from Araba.
"What's the matter, dear?" Araba quickly quips in, giving him a gentle caress on his shoulder before turning to the attendant.

"Let's take him back in."

She is rewarded with a supporting chorus, which eliminates any curiosity sparked by how she cut Angela off.

"He is still quite traumatised," the doctor says shortly afterwards, following close examination and finding no other material source of Toju's reaction. He then proceeds to sedate him for the journey home.

As soon as the drug takes effect, Toju is moved back into the car, but when Angela makes to take the seat beside the driver, Araba steps in.

BeGone | Temi Taiwo-Oni

"There will be no need for that, Angela. I'll take this from here," is all Araba says to Angela to deter her from tagging along. Taking her hint, like everyone else, Angela steps back and folds her arms across her chest, grumbling softly as the car zooms away conveying.

Araba places a call as the car bounces through a bumpy street with her husband's head bobbling sporadically across her lap.

"Hello, we just left the hospital." She pauses briefly. "I'll need your help with him, so please, meet us at home." She looks down at his limp face cradled against her midsection. "The way things are, you'll have to start work right away. Okay, bye."
Araba ends the call and stares at the listless form before her. A little later, the phone rings out unexpectedly, startling her for a second. Recognising the caller, she picks up the call.

"Hello... Hello, Marti... Yes, you remember now? That's good news. Can you call h... What! You want to send me his numb... Okay, the money I promised... Just send your account number and once you get it, send me the guy's number... Alright. Bye."

A half-smile forms on her lips as she relishes the prospect of getting her coveted sketchbook back. They are in the general vicinity of her house when she hears the beeping of her phone, and she checks to see Martin's text showing his account details. She gives directions to Onoja on how to get to the house, and just as she concludes the transfer, Onoja brings the car to a stop right in front of their gate.

A man is waiting by a green car just outside the house, and when Onoja steps down to open the gate, he approaches the vehicle. Araba winds down the window, tossing a probing look at the newcomer, who leans into the window.

"Mr Oche? The nurse I spoke to?" Araba's brow is arched upwards as she maintains her stare.

"Good morning, Madam. Yes, I am. I'm glad I arrived just in time." The tall, thickset man's voice is unusually hoarse, not quite husky for a man of his physique, yet, somewhat shrill.

"Perfect timing, please, come in then."

Onoja returns and sidesteps Oche to get into the car. He drives inside, and Oche follows on foot and helps to shut the gates. He then supports Toju, who is still blacked out, to the house, and into the spare room on the ground floor that Araba had prepared the day before since climbing the stairs would be a problem. Once they set Toju down, comfortably in the bed, Araba addresses Oche.

"Now that you've met your patient, let's discuss what you need to care for him."

Onoja looks eagerly at her as if expecting instructions, but he takes her cue and leaves when she pays him no mind.

"Madam, as discussed…"

BeGone | Temi Taiwo-Oni

"Mrs Cole will do just fine."

Oche downturns his mouth and looks pointedly at her before continuing.

"I reviewed the doctor's report you sent and will be here from seven a. m. daily till eight p. m. to assist with bathing, toileting, tracking vital signs, dispensing his medicines, assisting during his physio sessions, and executing other tasks based on the doctor's instructions about his care."

"Exactly what I need, as I'll be out of the house most of the time and need to attend to our babies. Here are his drugs."

Araba hands him a white nylon bag with navy blue fonts which read 'Teratai Hospital' in large print. She also draws a white sheet of paper from her bag, where the medicine prescriptions are listed. He is still reviewing it when she leads him out.
"Let me show you around the house since you will be practically living here for a while."

"I'll..."

The sound of the doorbell interrupts his response. She looks at her watch briefly, saying, "that must be Chii and the twins."
Araba hurries to the door, leaving a curious Oche slowly tailing her. She bursts out of the front door just as Onoja turns back from where he is standing by the gate, looking as if he meant to come inside to confirm access to the visitors.

"Madam, she says she is your friend an... "

"Yes, I'm expecting them. Please, let them in." She says, cutting short his inquiry. Smiling, she approaches the gate, craning her neck as he opens the gate to let in the visitors. She is halfway there when her two tots make a rush at her with shrieks of glee.

"Mommie! Mommieee!" They echo excitedly.
"My babies, Mummy missed you."

She stoops and snatches them into a warm, snugly embrace.

"Leave some hugs for us, o!" Chii's request is met with a smile, and when Araba looks up, one can almost see the invisible vibes of gratitude streaming between them.

"Thank you so much, Chii, you don't know it, but you saved a life."

"And if you keep harping about it, I just might send you a bill." They both burst into laughter as Araba responds.

"You kuku know that I cannot afford a posh madame like you."

She slides the girls down to the ground and takes each by the hand before pecking Chii on each cheek and brushing into a hug as close as possible. That's when she notices the last group member, standing metres away, between Onoja and Chii. She is a middle-aged woman, seemingly close in age to her, dressed in a simple Ankara gown, with a headscarf firmly tied to her crown.

Her torso aligns her hips and chest in an almost parallel manner. There is a friendly yet respectful flicker in her eyes as she draws closer.

"You must be Ndidi."
"Yes, madam. Good afternoon."

Extracting herself from Chii, she straightens up and acknowledges the newcomer before veering her head towards her friend to offer a new smile.

"You're just an angel, Chii! Welcome, Ndidi; let's all get inside."

By the time they make their way into the living room, Oche is leaning against the wall, somewhere close to the lounge.

"Girls, come and meet..."

"Is Toju back home yet?" Chii asks simultaneously, and upon hearing Chii mention their father's name, the twins burst into a chorus.

"Mommie, where's daddy?" The duo echoes cheerily, looking at their mother in anticipation.

"Your daddy is sleeping. He is still not feeling very..."

The girls immediately dash away from the group, like scurrying mice, towards the stairway,

"Girls, he is not in his room, and I told you, he's sleeping."

Araba lets out an exasperated sigh as Oche and Ndidi instinctively dart toward the children. It all happens so fast, to Araba's surprise, which quickly turns into amusement. She stiffens, widening her eyes, but a moment later, she lets out the breath that she did not know she had been holding and cradles her chest as if trying to keep it from crashing to the floor.

Sparkle, the meeker and more reserved of the two, ends up with Ndidi, while Oche's long legs quickly catch up with Rosie. He blocks her way and stoops to eye level with her before expanding his lips into a broad, friendly smile.

"Hi, little madam, won't you say hello?"

His raspy voice does not sound quite as scary with that smile tapered to his face. Gently and gradually, Oche charms up the little lady and walks her a few steps back to where her sister is standing with Ndidi. The girls take a moment to glance at their mother, and seeing her beam back at them, they gladly receive her okay to remain in present company. Soon, the quartet is settled in the corner, distracted but happily engaged in healthy banter.
"And that is Oche, the private nurse I hired to help with Toju. Anjola, my old classmate, who runs a medical consultancy in Abuja, called out of the blue two nights ago and helped me make the arrangements."

"Oh! I see," says Chii. "The same one who finally convinced you to get a nanny. I was surprised when you called to ask me to help get one, but I knew I'd get the details when I came by."

"I thought it through and felt a few things needed to change," Araba says. Her thoughts wander a little, and a smile fills her face, "It's long overdue."

The women catch up briefly as Araba shares the episode with Toju and the car before they left the hospital and her drama in the hospital two days ago.

"I'm so glad you're getting the help you need." Chii reaches out to her and grins. "People need people, and we all need support to lean on from time to time."

"Thank you, Chii. And you know, this also gives me a chance to get back into the business while Toju is incapacitated and recuperating and also start to do something for myself."
Chii narrows her eyes and pauses for an instant.

"Are you sure mister Tee will like that? I know you told me you worked together before, but it's been so long. You just don't seem like the type to sit in an office all day."

Chuckling, Araba shakes her head even as she holds up her right hand to say *No more*. When she collects herself, she clarifies Chii's assertion.

"Haba! I have no intention of sitting there full-time. I would get restless sef. After all, I'm not trying to wrest control from Toju. I'll just ensure I'm up to speed with the company's affairs, and it shouldn't be too hard, being that I was there for a while myself. In the meantime, I'll also find a productive outlet for my art skills. You remember that I'm an artist, right?"

"Really?" Gasping in surprise, Chii arches her brows, peering curiously at Araba. "I never would have guessed. I figured you studied Philosophy, or Igbo language, or something of a sort." She rolls her eyes, and they laugh light-heartedly.

The talk about being an artist reminds Araba about Martin and her sketchbook, so she makes a mental note to call him when they are all adequately settled in.

"Ha, Ha, very funny" Araba flicks her braids and smacks her lips at her friend." I'm a fine art major, FYI. Though I may be a tad rusty, I'll be tip-top again with a bit of practice."

"You seem to have it all worked out, anyway. That's great!" Her scepticism quickly drops as she senses the passion that Araba carries. She encourages, "with a little more time then, everything will work themselves out, and things will revert to normal."

Mentally protesting the pronouncement, Araba smiles and nods in feigned agreement.

Normal? I hope not. Not if I can help it.

The thought is as loud as if she said it, but Chii's lavish grin confirms that she did not. When from the corner of her eye, she sees Ndidi approach, she realises that the drama with the kids has made for an awkward start to her new arrangement. She looks beyond Ndidi to see the twins drifting off to sleep on a couch while Oche is nowhere in sight. Before she can ask, Ndidi explains.

"Madam, he said he was going to check their daddy."

She gesticulates in the direction of the room they had settled Toju into earlier. Spotting Ndidi's unpacked bag nearby, Chii takes it as her cue to let them settle in. She stands up, presents some excuse to leave, and gives Araba time to put her house in order.

BeGone | Temi Taiwo-Oni

Toju awakens to find himself lying in an unfamiliar bed, all by himself. He makes to sit up, but a wave of pain at the slightest movement makes him have second thoughts. When his vision sharpens, he realises that he is wrong on two counts. First, he is lying in the spare room in his own house as he recognises it, despite having not frequented it.

Also, he isn't alone. A hefty man is sitting close by, fiddling with his phone. They make eye contact when the man notices his wakeful state.

"Who are you, and why are you in my house?" Toju's intended challenge comes off as a weak accusation.

"You're awake, sir," Oche says, instinctively getting up. "I'm Oche, your nurse." Observing Toju's confused reaction, he continues. "Your wife hired me to take care of you."

"Nurse? Oh! Okay. But you're a...!" Toju's features soften slightly as he mentally puts the situation together.

"I know... I'm a guy. We are rare, but we do exist. Anyway, sir, your wife set you up here since taking you upstairs would have been herculean."

A smile lights up Toju's face.

"That shouldn't be a problem for you. You share his genes." Shaking his head slightly, Oche looks fleetingly confused.

"I share whose genes? I don't follow, sir."

Toju wears an impassive expression and looks Oche directly in the eye, making him unsure how to react toward his new patient.

"Hercules, undoubtedly."

Uncomfortable, he looks away, considering how to change the subject. In that instant, a snigger escapes from Toju's lips as his eyes widen in amusement, and before long, both men, patient and nurse, are quaking in amusement.

"A lovely sense of humour you have, sir. You must be feeling much better. I'm afraid you won't need my services as long as your wife expects."

Oche explains how he fits into the homecare arrangements and what Toju should expect and gives him his medicine as they chit-chat. The ease at which they get along convinces him that they will be okay. He finds it a much better experience than he usually expects from a male patient. In his previous experience, men are generally take a standoffish approach to their medical vulnerability as a defence mechanism.

Just as hunger pangs rap at Toju's hungry belly, squeals of childish chatter draw the pair's attention to the children outside the room.

Toju's heart lurches at the thought of seeing his toddlers, who he hadn't spared a thought about in the last few days.

"Are my daughters at home?"

He realises at this point that he has missed them.

"Yes, sir. Would you like me to get them?"

"Yes, please, if you don't mind, and perhaps some food, too. I'm starving."

The glint of humour exudes from his countenance before Oche leaves to fulfil his request. He is beaming with an easy grin by the time the trio arrive.

"Daddy!"
"Daddie!"
At the sound of their squeals, his hands begin to tingle, and he reaches out as far as he conveniently can. The adorable twosome breaks into his arms, attacking Toju with bear hugs. Initially, Oche watches from the doorway until the soft growl from his gut prods him to tend to his patient's second request and the plea of his hunger. Luckily, Ndidi has settled in and has lunch ready on Araba's instructions.

Despite his professed hunger, Toju spends almost a full hour cuddling and bonding with his daughters afresh. From some of their comments, Oche senses that they aren't used to spending alone time with him but sees that they are enjoying it. Later, when he is eating, he wonders what kind of person he was before the accident, sensing that he is somewhat different now from before the accident.

Araba's short visit afterwards confirms his misgivings. Oche has just led the twins to the living room to watch television and allow him to rest. The memorable scent of her aura hints at her advent before he opens his eyes or hears her movement. He smiles, genuinely happy to see her, but she looks away and avoids eye contact. Confused as to why his wife is guarded and uncomfortable around him, he speaks up.

"Are my scars so ugly that you can't bear looking at me, or am I so repulsive that you cringe at my touch?"

Araba peers curiously at him, uncertain about how to respond to his inquiry. Finding his actions strange and unsettling, she fears they may upset her rebellious plans to get back on her feet.

"I see you have met Nurse Oche. He says that he's explained our arrangement. I also hired a nanny for the girls since I no longer intend to sit back at home." Her words are flat and detached, devoid of affection or emotion.

"That's a great idea!" Toju's reply is exuberant and disconcerts Araba further. She arches an eyebrow at her husband.

Is this guy okay? Is this the same Toju?

As these thoughts flood her mind, she flinches, squishing her eyebrows together like she's seen a stranger or a ghost. She is incapable of processing her husband's jovial demeanour and his unexpected reaction to the knowledge of the steps she has taken. Toju has always loathed having household staff and only viewed the driver as an official amenity.

Indeed, before marriage, he had a cleaning lady who came in weekly while he maintained his meticulously tidy habits on his own. After they had gotten together, however, he had convinced her that they were better off taking care of their space on their own. His sister, Aunt Sylvia, had stepped in when the twins came along but returned to Belgium soon once they started crawling.

"You're not upset that there are outsiders in the house?" She cannot hide her surprise.
"Why should I be? They're here to help, aren't they?"
Ignoring the question, she offers a curt remark.
"Let Nurse Oche or Ndidi, the nanny, know whatever you want. I'll be resuming at Scentio tomorrow to take your place... for now" The last two words are said below her breath.

With that, she flees straight to her bedroom upstairs. She slams the door behind her with quivering lips and palpitations pulsing through her chest.

Left with the uncanny feeling that being nice to her upset her, Toju ponders his predicament.

PART 6

The next day, Araba promptly leaves for the office sometime after Oche arrives. At first, she feels awkward about leaving her children alone with two new people, but she consoles herself that they had gotten along with the children, and she suppresses the need to worry.

Gathering further comfort from her decision to have cameras installed in the house a day before Toju's return, she calls up the app on her phone to confirm that it's working.

Arriving at the office, Onoja drives straight to the main entrance of the building, signalling the security guards to open the door for her. Scanning the two-storey glasshouse where Scentio Industries' head office is housed, she mentally compares it to the warehouse that had housed both the office and the factory years back when she had just joined. Having been here only once, she is overcome by the apprehension that she may look conspicuous rather than exude confidence as she intends.

Nervously, she imprints a plastic smile on her face and glides up the entrance stairs into the lobby. Providentially, she is saved from the trouble of quibbling with the receptionist when Mr Benton and Wonu Maiye arrive at the reception from the lift.
"Mrs Cole, it's a pleasure to see you today. How is M. D. doing?" Wonu speaks up first, taking long strides to meet up with her motionless figure. He extends his hand, which she takes gladly, and replies.

"Good Morning, Mr Maiye. Toju is recuperating quite well." She turns to Mr Benton, who tucks his face to the fore of the group.

"Good morning, Mr Benton."

"Madam, you're welcome."

"The security informed us of your arrival via intercom, and to be fair, we weren't expecting to see you."

"Well, I'm here now, and if we go up to Toju's office, we can talk about why I'm here." She looks around before she lowers her voice a notch, saying, "out of the glare of staff."

Glancing around, Wonu and Mr Benton notice trickles of staff loitering around. Word has spread about her visit, and a few staff indulge their curiosity.

"Please, come this way, madam."

Mr Benton gestures towards the lift, leading the way. When the metal doors of the lift finally split open, Angela is the lone figure inside.

Angela's jaw drops slack when they spot each other, while Araba sucks in an inaudible gasp and tightens her face. Slapping on her plastic smile the next second, Araba locks her eyes on her husband's assistant.
"Err erm... Good morning, Mrs Cole... Good morning, sirs."
Angela recovers and jars her attention from Araba before making to slip out of the lift.

"Aha! Angela! Just the person I was hoping to see. Is M. D.'s office open?" Mr Benton is oblivious to the chemistry between the women and carries on like nothing is out of the ordinary.

"Errr! Yes, I always ensure it is cleaned daily and have it open so that I can easily access it if anything is needed at short notice."

"Isn't it risky to leave his office open?" Araba spins out her question inquisitively.

Angela becomes defensive immediately by squaring her shoulders and raising her voice slightly.

"I always lock my office, which is the primary access to his office. I am very professional in my duties."

"Well, that's good. Come with us. We need access in there right now." Wonu's comment reflects his amusement at the reaction from both women.

They make their way to the second floor, and Angela lets them into Toju's office. Although she intends to stay, Araba's blunt and derisive remark compels her to excuse them, and she leaves sporting a scowl.

Thank you, Angela. You can leave now.

After thudding the door to a close behind her, Angela echoes her words quietly. She strains to listen but can't make out the words because of the room's proofing. She remains at her desk, sullen and sulking. It's another forty-five minutes before the two men exit. She jumps to her feet immediately she sees Wonu Maiye, who just gives her a nod and struts out of the door.

"Mrs Cole will be in the office until Mr Cole gets back on his feet. Let her have everything she needs."
Mr Benton's directive is crisp but cordial since he is unable to divorce himself from his usual pleasant nature. Cleary, the meeting has not gone too well.

"Okay, sir! Yes, sir!" Angela responds straight away with a nod.

Once he is out of sight, she tiptoes to Toju's doorway and presses her ear against the door. Hearing nothing, she clutches the handle and knocks lightly.

Getting no response, she turns the handle and pushes the door. Well, she attempts to push it, but it doesn't budge, inducing more boldness in her. However, pushing harder and jerking the handle presents no success, causing her to ultimately give up and take her seat. Unsatisfied, she punches two buttons on the intercom and waits for it to ring, frowning as it drones softly. Then, she hears a click.

"Hello." Araba's tone is confident but soft.

"Madam, it's me, Angela. I was at the door to see if you need anything, but it's locked."

"Oh! I was in the restroom and didn't hear you knock. I'm fine, Angela. I need nothing for now. Thank you."
The call ends with another click, leaving Angela growling in displeasure and banging the phone unto its cradle.

"Arrgh!" Her growl is not loud enough to be heard outside her workstation.

Inside, Araba settles down to review the documents on Toju's table, and when she's done, she checks for the number sent by Martin. Calling immediately, she is a little giddy at the prospect of being close to retrieving her sketchbook. She places it on speaker and drops the handset on the table, staring at the screen anxiously, regretting the decision not to have Truecaller installed on her mobile. The ringing stops after the fourth, and she is quick to speak up.

"Hello..." Getting no immediate response, she clears her throat and speaks a little louder.

"Hello, good morning."

"Hello, who is this?" The speaker has a melancholy tone, but this does not discourage Araba.

"My name is Mrs Cole, and it appears you helped me find my sketchbook."

She surmises that it's better to be polite than make demands outrightly.

"Sketchbook? I don't know what you're talking about."

"No, you found it in an Uber you took. Martin was the driver; I got your number from him."

"Look, even if I saw a book or whatever, what gives you the impression that I'll hold on to something that's not mine?" Araba senses that he is being sly and resorts to pleading.

"See, I don't want any trouble. That sketchbook has sentimental value, and I need to get it back. Where did you drop... dump it?"

"I hear value and my ears sharpen, but, I'm sorry, I can't help you."

The line becomes dead as soon as he finishes speaking. When she dials again, it doesn't connect, and she is disheartened. She continues to try at intervals for the rest of the day, but it is all to no avail. It is early afternoon before Angela hears from Araba again on the intercom.

"Please, can you have Mr Onoja bring the car around? I'll be leaving shortly and can't reach him on his line. Thank you."

Another curt instruction but this time, Angela is ready as her professional mode is activated. She mechanically makes the call as instructed and advises Araba afterwards. When Araba leaves for the day, Angela barely spares her more than a cursory glimpse, and a nod, acknowledging her exit.

BeGone | Temi Taiwo-Oni

Araba feels tired during her ride home. Having spent most of her time shuttling between reviewing the reports sent by Wonu and following up on the lead Martin provided per her missing Sketchbook, she hasn't had much time to check the closed-circuit screens as planned.

Almost surrendering to a light nap while checking it, she suddenly sits up. Her eyes widen in shock as she sees an unexpected figure at the gate, stepping out of a black sports utility vehicle.

"Aunt Sylvia!" She gasps.
Her phone starts to ring instantly as the same name invades her screen.
"Madam?" Onoja slows down and offers a side-glance, "Did you say something?"
"No, just hurry home, we have an intruder... sorry, I mean guest."
"Okay, ma."
The ringing phone does not let up, and she sucks in a deep breath, swipes the green icon, and instinctively taps the speaker icon.
"Hello!"
"Hello, where are you? I'm outside your gate."
"Aunty! Ah! When did you arrive in the country? I'm heading home now. I wasn't expecting you!" A sense of de ja vu smacks her as she recalls the same retort being lashed at her earlier.
"Well, I was abroad, and now I'm here. Can you get someone to let me in? I need to see my brother!"

"Oh yes! I'll be there shortly. Someone will come now." Araba stutters as a feeling of dread swells across her chest.

"Good. I'm of no use abroad if my brother is mending in your care."

The inflexion in '*your*' emphasises the unhidden cynicism, and Araba quickly turns off the speakerphone, wary of being humiliated within the driver's earshot. Bumbling with placing the phone to her ear, she attempts a reply.

"I'll call..." There's a click, and then the line goes dead.
She hastily calls Ndidi to let Aunt Sylvia in and ensure that she is comfortable and treated well.

PART 7

Awakened by an unusual, noisy din, Toju is bothered, as it does not sound like the television or the children playing. At first, he assumes that Ndidi and Nurse Oche might be involved in an argument or discussion and blames his unfamiliarity with living around so many strangers.

He attempts to wander back to sleep as he is still tired from his session with the physiotherapist about an hour before. Oche had understood his need for rest and had left the room himself after getting Ndidi to take the children out.

His eyes flip open at the sound of a very familiar voice. His mind is befuddled as he tries to place who it is. Whoever it is, seems intent on gaining access to him and is heard arguing with Oche about seeing him.

"Madam, my patient is resting, and I can't wake him. He is exhausted from his therapy session."

BeGone | Temi Taiwo-Oni

"You have no right to stop me from seeing Toju. I'm his sister, and I flew in to take care of him, just as I have since he was a teenager." Toju's ears throb as he processes the discussion.
"Ma, I apologise, but you still cannot see him now. If he were at the hospital, you would res…"

"It's alright, Nurse Oche; let her come in." Toju's interruption causes both speakers to pause.

"Toju!" Aunt Sylvia rushes into the room and descends on him, enclosing him in a warm hug. As Toju groans at the sudden and severe embrace, Oche admonishes her.

"Madam, he has undergone two surgeries this week. Providence is the only reason he is home this soon, ma."
Realising that she may be hurting him, she loosens her grip and stands back to scrutinise him.

"Toritseju! *Ome mi bokoo? Ara de? Se ara ni e?*"
Toju appears a little baffled at her greeting and tries to cover up his instinctive reaction.

"Sister, welcome. I'm still a bit sore, but I'm much better than the first day." He starts to smile, but he holds back when she seems not to share the sentiment.

"You look so pale; I'm sure that your Raba has not been feeding you properly. Where is she, by the way?" Her eyes hover all over Toju, and then, she looks back towards the doorway.

BeGone | Temi Taiwo-Oni

"I can't eat properly yet as you know I had surgery. In any case, what I'm eating suffices for my recovery."

"Speaking of which, what really happened? How did this accident occur? No one has filled me in on this. All I know from social media is that you were at some bus stop, and a truck rammed into your car."

Toju shares the details he remembers about meeting up with his driver after driving himself in heavy traffic. Since he is yet to recall what happened after the driver arrived, he explains that he thinks that's when the accident occurred. She looks intently at him; her penetrating glare comes off as if she is trying to pierce through to his mind.

"There's something different about you. I can't place it, but I sense it."

Mildly irked at being the subject of such scrutiny, Toju turns away and begs off for some time to rest and owing to his persistence and perceived frailty, she obliges him, albeit reluctantly.
The girls are fresh from sleep when she gets into the living room, and in their innocent yet amiable way, they gladly latch on her as she shares with them some treats she has brought. Seeing her belongings perched on the floor beside the three-seater, she calls out to Ndidi.

"Where's that young lady? Can you please, take my bags inside? It is unseemly just to leave it lying around here."

Ndidi emerges while she is still speaking and looks blankly at her biting her lower lip. Her eyes stray to the staircase and then to the front door.

"Ma, I don't know where to put them, ma. Madam, no, tell me. Should I put them in the children's room for now, ma?"
"Well, that's a start!" Aunt Sylvia eyes her as she picks up the bags before turning back to the girls playing beside her. Minutes later, Ndidi brings a jug of water and a tumbler and sets them on the stool beside Aunt Sylvia.

"Would you like anything else, ma? Juice, tea... or something to eat?"
Surprised but unable to resist the offer, she looks up and replies in a calmer, more receptive tone.

"Tea would be nice, please."

Ndidi retrieves her tray and retreats to the kitchen, returning a few short minutes later with a jug of tea and a saucer of biscuits that she found in the kitchen.

BeGone | Temi Taiwo-Oni

When Araba arrives home some thirty minutes later, Aunt Sylvia is resting between the two babes, also dozing away. Ndidi is seated on the rug, away from the main living room area but jumps to her feet when she sights her madam.

"Welcome, ma."
"How are you?" Araba says and goes in the other direction towards the sleeping cluster.
"They're asleep, ma." Ndidi offers, causing Araba to pause her approach.
"Did you offer her anything... give her whatever she asked for?"
"Yes, Madam. I gave her tea and biscuits, and she shared with the children, ma."
"How about food? She didn't ask for anything else?"
"No, Madam... Em... She wanted me to put her bags inside, and when I didn't know where I put them in the children's room."
"That's okay. They rarely sleep there anyway. I guess she can have that room. How about nurse Oche?"
"He is inside with Oga."
Araba pokes her head inside the guest room, almost colliding with Oche, just at the door. They both react in unison.
"Hey!" Araba says, taking a step back.
"Sorry!" Oche opens the door wider and stands back to let her in.
"I was just about to step outside. Good afternoon, Ma'am."

"It's okay. How is my husband doing?"

"He is fine from the looks of things. No major improvements, but his attitude and cooperation show plenty of progress in the right direction. Many patients lack the grit to make it through recovery, and for a man, he has a pretty positive attitude about it."

"I wasn't asking for a medical report. A single statement that he is responding well would have sufficed."

Oche is stunned by her brusque rebuke and gives her a searching look while defending his position. "In that case, madam, he is responding well."

"Alright."

She studies Toju's sleeping form. With his features relaxed, he resembles the man she once knew. She turns around and leaves the room abruptly, saying nothing further to Oche. He shrugs, unable to reconcile being snapped at because of his feedback to her.

"Women! Must be her time of the month!" Mumbling under his breath, he takes his seat by Toju's side and picks up his phone.

Even as she climbs the stairs, shame descends on Araba for her unwarranted harshness towards Oche. Probing her conscience, she considers whether his tirade truly ticked her off or something else. Unable to pinpoint a single thing, she lists out all the things that got to her while she was there. First, her closeness to him seemed a little uncomfortable for her, with her husband and Aunt Sylvia being so close-by and he being just a few inches away from her.

Secondly, she has found that his voice is soothing, to an extent, and this is unnerving for the same reason. Next is his scent. Still trying to place it, she finds it stimulating in the most disconcerting yet thrilling way. She pauses her countdown to curb the discovery of something more.

Concluding that snapping is the least vile reaction that she could have had at the time, she acquits herself for doing so. However, shame is now replaced by guilt over her feelings.
Towards a nurse?
She cannot even explain what came over her, even to herself. Having worked in the past, with the combination of scents and striking men, it's a bit strange to feel this way. Blaming it on nerves from the day's stress and the last few days, she takes a shower, dresses up and joins the household downstairs, knowing that her impending confrontation with Aunt Sylvia cannot be delayed for much longer.
"Mommie!"

The echo of the youngsters lifts her spirits, and her morale instantly spikes.
"My babies! I missed you today. Hug! Hug!" Sweeping them close, she draws a deep breath, savouring their cuddle.
"Every child loves their mother, even a bad one. So, you now sneak in without greeting elders."
Aunt Sylvia's sarcasm taints the moment, causing her to detangle from them and focus on her.
"Good afternoon, Aunt Sylvia. You're welcome, ma. How was your flight?"

BeGone | Temi Taiwo-Oni

Pouted lips and an upturned nose are the response she gets, even before she is done speaking.
"My flight was just that, a flight to deliver Toju from your inattentive care. I just knew you would not take care of him."
Already used to the antagonism, Araba remains poised on the spot, holding onto the girls.

"Aunty, I got a professional to do it just so that he receives the best care."

"Hian! Professional! Is that what you call that one that did not want me to see my own brother. Professional indeed, he is."
Accepting that there is no winning with her sister-in-law, she changes the subject.
"I'm so sorry, ma. Would you like something to eat now?"
Aunt Sylvia snorts at her, appraising her before replying.
"Didi, or what's her name is getting me food. What I'm not okay with, is how my brother is being treated." She launches into a speech about how she expects her brother to be cared for and how she prefers to be treated by 'workers' in her brother's house.

Almost twenty minutes later, after having had her fill with the ridicule, Araba lashes out, interrupting the lecture.

"Aunt Sylvia, it's enough. I have heard what you have to say. Toju is fine and being taken care of, and I have no care for being talked down to in my own home. You are our guest and are welcome to stay as long as you remain cordial."
Unable to restrain herself, Aunt Sylvia pounces up and places both hands akimbo.

BeGone | Temi Taiwo-Oni

"Eweee! Araba!" she pronounces the name poorly on purpose. "Have you lost your mind? You dare speak to me in this way in my brother's house, you untrained *ngbaati* girl.

She makes to pounce on her with a slap, but Araba dodges it as she springs away.
"You dare not, Aunt Sylvia! Especially if you don't want to be disgraced in front of these little ones."
The two women cast glances at the girls, who, though seated by the television, are conscious of the rising tensions around them. Araba stares keenly at her antagonist, and with lips repressed into a straight line, she readies herself for what is to come. Curbing every iota of hesitancy she feels about following through with this stand-off, she squares her person and maintains eye contact.
Flummoxed, her adversary curls her lips into a snarl while her eyes bulge out of her sockets, appearing to double. She inhales deeply in succession as her nostrils flare with each exhale.

"*Wesi me gbe re? Ni ko we gbe yi wa?*" She utters an invective in Itsekiri, sweeping her gaze all over Araba. She makes to take a swoop at her when a male voice bellows in the background.
"That is enough, Sister!"
Toju!
Shock and relief drown Araba simultaneously as, despite standing up for herself, she knows there is no way a confrontation would not spiral out of control. Breaking eye contact, she looks to the doorway of the guest room to see Toju leaning between the door frame and Oche's shoulder.

Aunt Sylvia is equally shocked to see the pair as well, and walks up to them.

"Toju! I can see why you always changed the subject anytime I asked after this defiant girl during our calls. If you had told me, I would have come down to deal wi..."
"Sister! I said that is enough.... The defiant girl, as you call her, is MY WIFE!" His voice is no louder than before, but his tone's severity is unmistakable. Oche looks at his feet, willing himself away from the fiasco, as the room freezes in silence.
"Daddie!"
The twins run to encircle Toju's feet, inadvertently diffusing the situation. Araba lets out the breath she didn't know she had held, and, looking curiously at Toju briefly, she exits without another word to the kitchen. Toju tugs at Oche to help him get into the nearest living room sea and slumps into its cushions as the girls fall into his laps. Oche returns to the bedroom and quietly closes the door behind him, relieved to escape the awkwardness. Mortified by the affront, Aunt Sylvia makes her way back to her seat to mull over the palaver since she has nowhere else to go.

BeGone | Temi Taiwo-Oni

That night, as Toju reclines in bed, he is plagued by flashes of startling images. One of them is a more vivid version of the one he saw while at the hospital. He is in the same room as before, and he sees now that it's his living room, and the heap on the floor is his wife, Araba, who is lying motionless. This image is preceded by one in which he strikes her, blow after blow, while she attempts to block and dodge his assault.

His heart throbs in unison with his actions in the flashback and in alarm at what is happening. He sees himself advance toward her, and how he uses his shoes to nudge her before walking away.

"Araba!"
The name escapes from his lips as he is lost in his nightmare.

How could I have walked away?
How could I have even attacked her in the first place?

His troubled soul breaks out from his slumber, sweating and distraught. His shoulders are pulsating as he heaves heavily, breathing deeply with each breath. Trepidation, at such an occurrence ever taking place, torments his being. He tries to calm down, compelling himself to believe that it's a bad dream, blaming the foiled onslaught by his sister as a trigger. He reaches for the glass of water on the bed stand and gulps it down in full slurps.

Contemplating the events in the nightmare for the next half-hour, it takes time for him to calm down and release himself to the lure of sleep. He, however, barely gets any tonight because the nightmarish imageries do not cease. He sees different scenarios where he is in confrontations with Araba. Restless through the night, by the time the first cracks of dawn streak through the sky, he is sombre, having cried in his spirit, the only way a man can.

Ashamed at what he now knows to be recollections of incidents over the years, he cannot look Araba in the eye when she stops by to check on him on her way to the office. As soon as she steps into the room, he turns his face away and refuses to make eye contact.

Thinking he has had a rethink about standing up for her last night, Araba narrows her eyes in renewed contempt and dashes out of the room, barely ramming into Oche, who has just arrived for the day.

Proactively, Oche steps aside just in time, wondering at a second near-miss collision. He makes a mental note to avoid standing directly in front of doorways when she is not in sight.

The two men hear her leaving instructions with Ndidi briefly before the loud slam of the front door announces her departure. With no sign of Aunt Sylvia, Toju figures that she is still smarting from the incident and is convinced that it must have taken its toll on her, causing the typical early riser to rouse late.

Toju is tight-lipped and melancholic all morning when Oche tries to engage him. The furrow along Oche's forehead signals to Toju that his silence triggers concern. At first, the nurse continues to carry out his duties casually, but afterwards, the inevitable questions arise.

"Are you sure everything is okay, sir? You're unusually quiet today, a drastic change from the last two days."
Oche's inquiry is conversational but coated with a professional edge.

"I'm alright."
Toju shuts his eyes, feigning sleep, but since he has just had breakfast and it's barely ten in the morning, Oche is not fooled.
"Sir, besides giving you your medications and helping with your physical care, part of my duties includes monitoring your physiological and psychological progress so that I can provide updates to the doctors daily."

Toju flicks his eyes open and eyeballs Oche. He weighs his next words carefully, conscious of divulging too much information.
"I slept poorly. I had nightmares, and I think they were real events, but I don't want to talk about them." His delivery is calm but glazed with pain as he winces with each word spoken.
Oche's response bites off some of Toju's defensive fences.

"Well, for starters, that's proof of recovery. Better the return of your memory than gaps that you can't account for, for the rest of your life."
Some memories are best forgotten.
Toju disagrees with this last bit, but he keeps his thoughts to himself.
In the meantime, Aunt Sylvia's voice is heard from the living room as Ndidi sorts out her late breakfast. In a bid to steer clear of her,

Oche seals the door and opts to end the discussion, but he notes the development in his report.

Devising a strategy for preventing any more skirmishes with Aunt Sylvia, he plans to keep his distance from her during his stay at the house. He effectively does this on the two occasions they run into each other later in the day.

BeGone | Temi Taiwo-Oni

The drive to work is tortuous for Araba. She doesn't know how to handle the situation with her husband. His defence of her is a first after so long, and checking him this morning with mixed feelings, backfired as his reaction put her off. The mess with Aunt Sylvia is another kettle of fish, but she had it coming. Upon her arrival at the office, she monitors the activities of everyone at home from her phone, as she is sceptical about what might happen today.

Meanwhile, Angela is unable to contain herself, as seeing Araba replace Toju in the office is something she finds hard to deal with. Feeling a little redundant, she can't contain her curiosity about what goes on in the office.

"I wonder what the woman does in there every day," she says to Ebun, her friend, one of the company's accountants, during the lunch break on Araba's second day.

"Why don't you go inside to find out yourself?" Ebun is lightly bemused by her friend's frustration.

"I would if I could," Angela says, frowning while sipping her smoothie. "She is too... I don't even know the right word to describe her. On the two occasions that I tried to check in with her yesterday, the door was locked. Today, I went in shortly after she met with the heads, and she quickly dismissed me, like I was intruding or something."

BeGone | Temi Taiwo-Oni

Gushing with laughter, Ebun covers her mouth to prevent her toast from spilling out. She dunks a mouthful of water down her throat and responds to Angela.

"This babe, please, no-kill me, abeg! Maybe you are intruding then. If it looks like a fish, it's most likely a fish. Duhhhh!"
"Mschew! Na, you know."
"I'm serious. I mean, it gives you a little free time. I mean, I could do with some free time myself right now. My workload has been a bit heavy since Idara travelled for her Masters."
"Well, that is you. I'm not wired to like free time. I like the activity and tension the job gives and keeping me idle is like pushing me over the railings. Anyway, that is not my biggest frustration, and if she likes, she should be an ice queen. My own is that I can't reach Oga Toju, and I'm worried about him."

"Ehen, ehen! You have just said what's doing you." Ebun eyes her mischievously. "You are missing your crush."
Angela smacks her on the arm but flushes in embarrassment.
"He is not my crush." Her retort comes out weak and less irate than she would have liked it to be.
"Why are you worried? He is in good hands, isn't he? He is at home with his family."
Angela opts not to respond and takes another sip from her drink.
"Okay, why don't you call him in that case?"
"Call ke? Do you think I haven't tried? His number is switched off, and it's so been since the accident."
The door to the lunchroom opens, and they see the bald head of Mazi, the only other accountant they had.

"Ebun, the boss wants you in his office now." He says it flatly and shuts the door as deftly as he had opened it. Ebun stands up sharply and begins to clear her dishes.

"Babe, I've got to run. If you are so concerned, go to his house or something and stop sulking all over." She grabs her lunch bag and blows Angela a kiss.
"If I were you, I'd bask in the light load and make the best of it. Be creative. I'm sure that you can think of something."
"But... even Onoja hasn't seen him since the day he drove them home from the ho..."
"Think of something!" Ebun is firm as she winks at her and closes the door behind her.
Angela stares at the door for several minutes after Ebun's departure, mulling over her advice. Her phone starts ringing, and looking at the caller's name, a smile breaks on her face. It's Aunt Sylvia.
"Hello, ma... I'm fine, thank you, ma... are you back in Lagos? That was fast, where are you... Oh! I see." Angela adjusts her seating and crosses her slim legs.
"You'd like me to come over to the house? Certainly! I'll come in tomorrow. I'll call when I'm on my way... Alright, ma. Bye."
Gradually, through the phone call, her lips spread into a wide grin. Providence, it appears, has gifted her the perfect solution to her dilemma. For the rest of the day, her disposition is generally lively, to the extent that she even smiles at Araba when she leaves at the close of business.

PART 8

BeGone | Temi Taiwo-Oni

It is a quiet Saturday morning in the Cole household and Toju's first weekend home. Though the details of the accident are presently removed from the members of the household, none of them can evade the realities of its aftermath, not even the little tots. After the departure of the physiotherapist, Toju wears a generally glum look, like a man who has found a thousand Naira and lost a thousand dollars.

Efforts made by his sister to harvest words from him are met with a distant and cagey mien. She is confused as to why her only sibling refuses to speak to her but is relieved to have reinforcement on the way. She quietly kicks her heels since she is still reeling from Araba's forward behaviour.

When Angela rings the bell, Araba, who is upstairs playing with the twins, is unsettled at the intrusion. Her resumption at the office had reined in any ceremonial gestures of commiserative visits by staff. Everyone knows Toju is a private person anyway, so no visits were expected per se.

Equally jolted by the doorbell, Toju's sister rushes out and quickly instructs Ndidi to let her guest in. Oche retreats from the living room where he has been chatting with Ndidi to Toju's side, hoping to evade any more drama. Araba peeks down from the top of the stairs.

"Ndidi, please, get the door. I'm not expecting anyone, so don't just let anyone in." Araba confidently dishes out the order, oblivious to the prior instruction. Ndidi is nowhere in sight, but she sees Aunt Sylvia standing alone downstairs, looking towards the doorway and bearing an impish look.
"Ndidi! Ndidi!"
Narrowing her eyes in the direction of Toju's sister, she bites her lower lip before returning to her room. Spotting one of the cameras she'd had installed, she hisses quietly and hurries to check her phone to see who is visiting. Just in time, she sees Ndidi letting Angela into the premises, prompting her chest to constrict forcefully. Biting the insides of her cheek, she resists the urge to tear downstairs, instead choosing to distract herself by paying attention to Sparkle's storytelling.

Downstairs, Aunt Sylvia makes a show of hugging and greeting her guest, loud enough to be heard upstairs. She ushers her unto the three-seater and continues her act.
"Angela! It's so good to see a friendly face." Angela crosses and uncrosses her legs and takes sidelong glances, despite keeping her head trained on her companion.
"Is my boss doing alright? You sounded frantic when we spoke yesterday."

BeGone | Temi Taiwo-Oni

Aunt Sylvia looks around to see if anyone is visibly within earshot before whispering, "hmmm! You won't believe the nerve of her... challenging me? Short of physically assaulting me... I mean, who does that?"

Angela covers her mouth dramatically as her eyebrows invert in feigned astonishment, suppressing her eagerness to see Toju, rather than this chit-chat. Leaning in, she keeps her gaze transfixed as Aunt Sylvia goes into details. While the gist is on, Ndidi surfaces with a tray stocked with a flask, teacups, and a plate of biscuits, along with some milk and honey. A hush settles over them when she arrives beside them, and they both utter thanks to her.

Aunt Sylvia has barely resumed her chatter when Toju materialises in the doorway of his temporary room, with Oche's support. Toju is casually dressed in a pair of chinos shorts and a T-shirt when Oche leads him towards a chair.

"Mr Cole!"

Angela shoots up as soon as she sights him and scurries to hug him. The awkwardness of the hug, as the three of them are locked together, knocks Angela back to reality, and she takes a step backwards. Oche observes the weird look exchanged by the duo and helps Toju into the seat before leaving.

"I thought to come out rather than receiving visitors indoors."

"How have you been, sir. We have been quite worried at the office, especially as Madam... I mean, your wife has taken to coming to the office after your discharge."

Aunt Sylvia takes that moment to jump back into the discussion.

"I have just been telling Angela how you have been holed up in the room, more often than not."

"That's not altogether true. I have been moving around during my daily physio sessions and spending some time with the girls. Where are they, by the way?"

A scowl registers on Aunt Sylvia's face as she responds to his inquiry.

"They're probably with their mother, upstairs. Why don't I go and get them while you two catch up? I'm sure she has updates for you to sort out."
Two pairs of eyes trail her exodus before they collide.

"It's good to see you up and about, sir," Angela says, ogling at him reticently.
"I'm glad to be alive."
"Most certainly, sir. We all are glad about that. The whole office was in turmoil when the news broke out on social media. I'm glad we arrived at the scene on time."
"Oh! You were there?" Toju squints as he tries to jog his memory.
"Yes, sir. We brought an ambulance to the scene, and I rode with you to the hospital."
Toju shuts his eyes, and flashes of his bumpy ride amid the pealing ding of the siren becloud him. Spasms quiver visibly through his arms and upper body.
"Are you alright, sir?"
"I remember, now... though it's not a pleasant memory. Tell me more about that day or whatever information you garnered."

"Akugbe told those who visited him that he had called you and agreed to meet up with you because you had complained about the traffic. He said that he had just gotten into the car when the accident occurred. His story is consistent with the report that the car was not in motion when it happened."

"Ahh! Akugbe! How is he doing? I have to reach out to his family."
"Actually, sir, he is doing much better, though he has a myriad of bruises on his body. He was discharged before you were. He is still on medical leave right now, though."
"Please, get me his…" It occurs to Toju that he no longer has a phone. That thought pieces together a portion of the feeling of inadequacy he has been experiencing.
"Angela, was my phone recovered from the scene?"
Angela's face drops as she realises her gaffe.
"No, sir, it wasn't. When we picked you up, our priority was saving your life. I apologise for that mistake."
She shakes her head and rubs her hand against her forehead.
"It's okay. You did the most important thing. You saved my life."

Angela breaks into a flush and looks away.
"I need you to do me a favour. I need to retrieve my line. I guess the focus around here has been skewed towards my recovery. And, you're the best person to resolve the retrieval, anyway. In the meantime, get me another line to use tentatively, and a new phone, of course."
"Certainly, sir. I'll sort it out today."
"Good"
"Nice to see you cheery and chirpy." Aunt Sylvia is descending with the kiddies in tow when she interrupts.

Toju throws a broad smile, holding out his arms to the twins, while Angela stands, watching the display.

"I'll take my leave now. Let me deal with the things you asked for."
"Ah-ah! How can you be leaving already?" Aunt Sylvia sounds disappointed as she frowns and slumps her shoulders.
"I'll be back, ma. I have an errand to run, ma."
Her face lightens up at the feedback, and she beckons her, encircling her into a firm grip before she bids her farewell.
"Alright, my dear. Hurry and be back soon."
Angela takes her leave, and Aunt Sylvia holds her chin high, letting out a gratifying sigh.

Later in the day, the house breaks into a flurry of activities as if Angela tipped off the world of his existence and need for social interaction. Wonu Maiye shows up first, with his wife, followed an hour later by the CEO of Scentio's biggest raw material supplier.

Araba is forced to step up as she comes downstairs and has Oche watch the children. Unprepared for the bevy of guests that flood the house, she tries to contain her frustration, switching automatically to her old perfect wife role. Even a keen eye would not notice any lack of chemistry between the couple. The only times Araba flinches are when Angela returns with the new phone for the first time and when Aunt Sylvia makes a biting remark about Toju being lonely and abandoned before her arrival.

With the return of a functional phone for Toju, he seems to become better engaged over the next few days. Araba's main relief is the children's resumption to school the following Monday, as it keeps them away from home for most of the day. On one occasion, when Aunt Sylvia attempts to ridicule her, Toju is quick to stand up for her and is almost gruff with his sister.

"Aunt Sylvia, Araba is my wife. You will accord her the same respect you do, me."

His sister does not take his chastisement lightly and tries all she can to wheedle her way back into his heart. She continues to suspect foul play because he had always sided with her in the past.

Araba, on her part, clings to her reservations about his change in attitude regarding her. She can't shake the memories of the abuse she has been through with him, and it continues to haunt any feelings of affection brewing between them.

She does, however, feel concerned over his refusal to eat better despite Oche and Ndidi's best efforts. Ndidi suggests one day that perhaps he would eat something prepared by Araba, but Aunt Sylvia takes to making his meals in her place. Notwithstanding this, her efforts fail to get him to improve his eating habits, but she keeps trying.

However, the pretence to the world that life has returned to normal, eats at Araba, and she cannot keep it up. She breaks into tears on Wednesday night, exasperated by her inability to keep going. Lying in bed, she mumbles her thoughts through her sniffles.

"I'm right back where I started, except for the beating—pretending to the world and hiding how I truly feel. Facing scorn, even though it's Aunt Sylvia this time, but scorn all the same, yet I hold it all in like nothing's happened. Maybe I should have run away. Maybe... maybe I should still run... just run... and for real, this time".

As the thoughts cement in her consciousness, she recalls the sight of seeing Angela on the closed-circuit screen, flinging herself on Toju and in their home, for that matter. She wonders if she is being made a fool of or if she is the one making a fool of herself.

Rosie stirs beside her, prompting her to stroke her gently back to sleep. After that, she shakes off the doleful musing and replaces it with thoughts of her children before snuggling them closely and nodding off to sleep.

When she awakens the following day, she is surprised to see Toju seated on a chair in their room, looking intently at her. Startled, she imagines that she's dreaming because of her final thoughts before sleeping off. Hence, she sits up sharply in the bed and peers carefully at him.
"I'm so sorry to scare you, dear." Toju is sweaty and looks menacing, as his lean, almost lanky form doesn't improve his appearance.

Araba studies him using the streaks of sunlight from the partly drawn bedroom curtain. The stubble on his chin which, in another circumstance, would have been found attractive, gives him a peculiar look because of the bruises mingled with them, something she has not taken note of before now. She has barely looked at him since they returned from the hospital, although she observes that yet another change has come over him since their encounter the other night. His hands are quaking, so he wrings them together to nip the quivers. His eyes seem to be staring beyond her as he continues to speak.

"I was restless and couldn't sleep, so I tried my hands at some of my physio exercises, then attempted the stairs. I made it halfway, and then... here I am."

He waves his hands in the air and then wilts. Warily, Araba looks at him, fearing that he would break into an outburst at any time. Toju detects the fear in her eyes and droops further into his seat, avoiding her eyes and pinning his arms to his sides.

"Was I that terrible... a monster?"

She opens her mouth to utter a response, then seals the lower lip with the upper one while shutting her eyelids in the same motion. When she looks up, she strains to make eye contact with him but gives up when she realises that he will not yield.

"I remember everything, Araba. At first, it came to me in flashes... nightmares that won't stop. Last night... overnight, they flowed in torrents. I couldn't stop them."

He finally looks up and takes his turn to search her eyes.
"Why didn't you tell me? Why didn't you?" His exclamation is like a wounded bear, causing her to cringe and draw up the duvet in defence.

Seeing his effect on her, Toju lets out a grunt of pain and flees the room as fast as his fragile body allows. He hears the lock click behind him as he slithers down the staircase, not pausing till he gets to the foot of the stairs. Surveying the living room, his gaze settles on the bar and immediately, he indulges his reflexes by heading towards it. Minutes later, his trudge to the room finds him armed with a glass cup and a bottle of Absinthe, the trophy spirit gifted to him during his last trip to France in March.

I can't stand this pain. I need to end this.

Its bitter-sweet taste hits his tongue first before the spicy aroma assaults his senses. He resists the urge to hold back, instead, he clings to the will to numb his emotions.

Sip after sip, he glugs the novelty drink, despite the alarm bells resounding in his head, and by the time Oche arrives about forty minutes later, the bottle is drained to almost half, while his glass is completely empty. He lies wasted on the chair with his bowels drenched with his problems and topped with the noxious fluid. Upon opening the door, the air holds a rancid stench, and Oche immediately knows something is up.

The uncovered bottle and used glass tell him all he needs to know, so he quickly rushes to check if Toju is still alive. He finds a pulse but realises that Toju is unconscious. He quickly turns him to his side, deftly executing the Bacchus manoeuvre and keeping his frame aligned.

Oblivious to all this, Araba, dressed to leave home, is descending the stairs, hoping to avoid Aunt Sylvia and Toju before leaving. Thoughts about the weirdness of the episode at dawn still cause her to shrink, sprouting doubts about her safety and Toju's sanity. She is not ready to discuss it and wants to maintain her distance from Aunt Sylvia.

As she takes the final step to the ground floor, Oche barges out of the room and almost bumps into her. She is flustered and serves him a questioning look, with one eyebrow askew and upturned while the other almost meshes with her eyelid.

"What is the matter?"

"Madam... er... good morning." The apprehension in his voice is unmistakable, and he rubs each thumb against his fingers as if in restraint. "I was just going to ask Ndidi to call you. Your husband has passed out... I think he overdosed on alcohol."
He turns back, expecting her to follow him to assess Toju, then halts when she remains rooted to the spot.
Hesitating, she experiences a sense of nostalgia, recalling that this is precisely how she felt when Angela called about the accident.

"Passed out? I saw him barely an hour ago, and he even climbed upstairs."
Flapping his hands eagerly, Oche gesticulates towards the room. "Come and see for yourself. That's how I found him."
They both proceed to the room, with Araba taking cautious steps, dreading what she might see.

"He was lying on his back when I found him, but I have done the only thing that can be done right now; I turned him to his side. I can't try to wake him as this might cause complications."
Warily, she examines Toju's features, seeing a calmer version of the stranger she saw this morning. Recognising the bottle at his side, she picks it up and studies it.

"He got this from France this year... a souvenir, he called it. He doesn't even drink that much. Is he going to be okay?" She raises her brows in askance, "could he have taken drugs?"

Oche collects the bottle from her and shakes his head.

"I found no evidence of drugs around, but we can't tell. However, I have already taken a look at this drink. Its alcohol concentration is quite high; sixty per cent. I'd have said we should take him to the hospital, but it's not advisable to move him. We'll just have to wait it out, but if you're worried, you can call the doctor and have him on stand-by."

At that moment, Aunt Sylvia waltzes into the room.

"Eh! Toju dear, what would you like to..."

Seeing Oche and Araba standing next to Toju conversing, she is taken aback.

"What's happening? What are you doing to him?"

The pair look up and Araba lets out a sigh.

"Toju... Oche found Toju like this. We think he got drunk on..."

"Got drunk ke? We both know Toju drinks light. What have you done to him?"

Araba shakes her head and steps back as Aunt Sylvia pushes her way past them to fuss over Toju.

"Good morning, ma. No one did anything to him. He needs to be left alone until it wears out."

She turns to Oche and eyes him sceptically before resting her eyes on his companion.

"Look, the two of you, I don't know what nefarious plans you have for my brother, but I won't let you get away with it."

They both gasp in amazement at her accusation. Oche's temples pulse as he clenches his jaw, containing his emotions. Araba readies herself for a shouting match but is interrupted by the spluttering to life of the sleeping figure.

Coughing and choking, he instantly douses the rising tensions, and they all scramble to pay him mind. As Araba lifts his head to cradle it, Toju inadvertently vomits all over her. Recoiling, she leaps back, but it's too late, as the liquid has drenched the front of her outfit. Disgusted, she flees from the room while Aunt Sylvia chuckles in mild amusement over her discomfort before helping to clean Toju up.

BeGone | Temi Taiwo-Oni

About two hours later, the women of the Cole household gather in the living room, having left Oche to tend to Toju. The Cole women sit in adjacent seats while Ndidi is at her usual spot away from them but primed to lend a hand to their needs. Ndidi is aware of the incident that happened in the morning because she had seen Araba bundling off and joined in cleaning up the room.

In addition, she had managed to pry some details off Oche in the brief moments they had alone. The girls have left for school without their ritual morning hug with their father, and now, watching the chemistry between the two women, she can sense everything else she was not told earlier. There have been no visitors today because Araba had instructed her to inform Onoja not to let anyone in, except on special instruction.

Toju has just woken up a second time and is now discussing the incident with Oche.

"I don't know what came over me. I find it hard to believe that I did all those terrible things that I saw in my flashbacks. And she was so scared of me when I went to talk to her about it. I just felt I should end it and relieve her of the misery."
"May I speak freely, sir?" Oche is wary of crossing boundaries or offending Toju.
"Go ahead."

BeGone | Temi Taiwo-Oni

"You see, if anything had gone wrong with what you did, you probably would have made things worse for her... and you won't be here to protect her."

He then shared what his sister had said to them and how things were about to spiral out of control the very minute before he regained consciousness.

"You see, we are a product of our past, but we don't have to stay in that space. I believe your accident is your second chance to start afresh. Use your pain to get back in line. Let it help you to be an improved version of yourself. All isn't lost just yet."

Toju nods in agreement, making a wistful side-glance as his countenance brightens up.

"You need to ask for her forgiveness. I see how she acts around you like she is angry and can't stand to be around you, yet," Oche's voice thickens, "I know she has compassion for you."

Toju becomes glassy-eyed and brings his gaze to meet with Oche's.

"Can she ever forgive me?"
"Now, that's a question that begs an answer. Ask her. She's the only one who can do it anyway, and if you don't ask, you won't know."

A gentle tension ensues as Toju struggles with his emotions, but it's gone in the next moment.
"You didn't see her face this morning. And on top of that, I get drunk and spew all over her. It's sickening, to even me."

Oche puts a hand on Toju's shoulder. "Give her a chance to speak for herself. And guess what? Even if she rebuffs you, give her time and ask her again. With what you've told me, you did not get to this point in one day. Give it time. Give her time, and... the rest will work itself out."

"Thanks, you are quite insightful for a single man your age."
Oche smiles weakly.

"What can I say? My parents had it tough for a long time, but I watched things improve, just when it seemed, there was no salvaging their marriage. It takes some work, but it can work out well."
Toju stretches out his hand, and the men exchange a firm, reassuring handshake.
"Thank you."

PART 9

BeGone | Temi Taiwo-Oni

It's past one o'clock in the afternoon when the bell goes off. Confident that Onoja would take care of whoever it is, everyone remains unperturbed. Shortly afterwards, Bob Marley breaks out into his tune, and Araba reaches for her phone. It's Angela. Instinctively, she remembers that she did not call in about not coming in today.

Figuring out she is the one at the door, she cuts off the call and instructs Ndidi to tell Onoja to let her in.
By the time Angela strides inside, Araba is on her feet, not too far away from the stairs.

"Good afternoon, Madam."
"Hello, Angela. Welcome. I forgot to mention that my plans changed, and I had to stay back home today." Then she mummers under her breath. "But I'm sure you've already been updated."
"Sorry, Ma'am?" Angela struggles to piece together the bit she did not hear.

BeGone | Temi Taiwo-Oni

Araba purses her lips, plastering on a smile and shaking her head, before waving Angela towards her sister-in-law. Then she proceeds upstairs. Angela joins Aunt Sylva on the three-seater, and the two are soon chattering away.
Abruptly, Aunt Sylvia interrupts Angela mid-sentence and jerks, exclaiming.

"Wow! Time has gone o! I need to get Toju's lunch." She heads for the bedroom and then turns back and nods at Angela.
"Come in and say hello, now." She signals for her to follow her in, and then enters the room.
Needing no further urging, Angela follows reluctantly behind her.

"Will you try the rice and beans, or you'll stick to the oats and bananas? You have to eat something nourishing. You have taken just tea all day."

Aunt Sylvia is speaking to Toju when Angela comes in, and Oche exits, giving them the room. Toju sighs and shuffles his eyes between the two women.

"Good afternoon, sir."
"Hello, Angela." He turns to his sister. "I'll take the oats, sister. I don't care much for proper food right now.
"Okay, let me get you a bowl..."
"No, o! A small cup will do. Let me crawl before I run, please."
Aunt Sylvia smiles and leaves his side.
"Why don't you stay and keep him company?"

149

Looking tentatively at Toju and back at Aunt Sylvia, Angela takes a seat beside him. Aunt Sylvia steps out, leaving the door slightly ajar.

Initially, an uneasy silence hovers between them as Toju is still depressed about how to handle the situation with his wife, and Angela realises that this is her first time alone with her boss after taking him to the hospital. Toju eventually starts a conversation on some obscure topic and beats the uneasiness.

Eager to make the best of the time with him, especially after noticing the sadness behind his eyes, Angela is genuinely moved to help him. She deliberately throws anecdotes into their conversation, causing Toju to lighten up and laugh after a while. They get so carried away that they do not notice Araba, standing at the doorway watching them.

She has just gotten a call regarding the recovery of her sketchbook and is headed out, but when she hears the laughter, she pops over to see what is going on. After a minute of watching them unnoticed, she quietly backs away and leaves the house. She collects her car keys from a surprised Onoja, urging him to stay and assist with any needs of the household.

BeGone | Temi Taiwo-Oni

She breaks down in tears as she makes her way to her destination. Unable to hold her emotions together, she is compelled to park somewhere and lets out her tears.

Toju, why do you continue to torment me in this way? Haven't you done enough? I don't know how to love a man like you, and I don't want to live like this.
The questions sweep unimpeded through her mind until Bob Marley sings on cue.
Could you be loved...
"Why the heck have I stuck to this damned ringtone?"
The egg-roll hawker strolling towards her car notices her animated outburst as she throws her hands in the air, so he gawks at her, offering her an odd expression. Ignoring him, she digs out her phone and taps the screen twice before dropping the phone on the dashboard.

"Hello Araba, how are you?" Chii's soothing voice oozes into the car's atmosphere, and like a breath of fresh air after being stuck underwater awhile, it is refreshing to Araba. Sniffing and drying her eyes with a handkerchief, she calms down.

"Hi, Chii."
"Hmmm! That voice again. Are you okay, Araba?"

BeGone | Temi Taiwo-Oni

"I'm fi... No! I'm not fine." Araba is herself surprised by her response.

"What's the matter? I take it from your hoarse voice that you've been crying or something."

"To be honest, Chii, I'm sick and tired of hiding behind the make-up. I am not fine, and I have not been for years. And... I don't think I can hold up anymore. Everything is just too much to deal with. I thought I could turn things around, but..."

"Hold on, dear. Take it easy. Can we meet up? This doesn't seem like a phone discussion. I'm doing school-run by myself today and was going to offer to help pick the girls. Is that okay?"

"Thanks so much Chii." Araba's voice is slightly calmer and more composed. "I was going to ask Onoja to do that. Let's meet at your house instead. I have a quick appointment somewhere in G.R.A. I'll come when I'm done."

"No problem, dear. Just hold yourself together, and we'll talk, ehen?"

They exchange farewells and end the call. Switching the car back into gear, Araba places her phone in the phone holder of the car and drives off.

That night, after the children have retired, Araba sets out to execute her new strategy. Her talk with Chii had been comforting but coupled with new matters arising in her life; her mind is made up, so she begins to pack up her things. She is grateful that many of the twins' clothes are already in her room since Aunt Sylvia has already taken over their room. It takes her over an hour and a half, but all their bags are packed by midnight. At the crack of dawn the next day, she has Ndidi take the bags to her car, and she quickly gets the girls ready for school.

When they are about to leave, Rosie wanders to Toju's recovery room.

"Rosie, come back here. We have to go."

"I want Daddie... kiss, kiss."

Letting out a sigh of frustration, she asks Ndidi to take Sparkle along so both girls can kiss him because she remembers that they missed it yesterday morning. Unfortunately for her, Toju, who is now feeling much better, stands up to see the girls out and sees Araba. She scrutinises him, wondering if he suspects anything. He watches them from the entrance of the room as they march out of the house.

When they get outside, Araba asks Ndidi to go back into the house to get her things as she is coming with them. Bewildered, Ndidi does as she is told and goes back in to get her things. When she returns minutes later, Araba has strapped in the girls and is seated in the driver's seat. Toju appears at the doorway as Ndidi opens the gate to let them out. He watches them leave sadly but does not voice out his protest.

The couple makes eye contact just before Araba drives out, but she looks away in guilt and pretends she doesn't see the sadness in his eyes. Ndidi is about to shut the pedestrian gate when Onoja arrives at the entrance for the day's work. Speechless, he catches the gate before it slams and watches on as she dashes into the front passenger seat before the car zooms off.

Epilogue

BeGone | Temi Taiwo-Oni

It's been three months since that Friday morning when Araba grabbed the children and left Toju. Sitting in her new office, she admires the pictures of the girls standing on her table. She shares the office with six other people, creatives like her at Ikigai Elements, an advertising agency, but she does not mind.

It's nothing compared with having her independence. Her phone chimes quietly and she smiles as she picks it up to check the message that she has just received.
It's a credit alert from her Bank.
Toju!
Since her departure, Toju has been sending periodic payments to her bank account, money she hasn't touched. One Million Naira. That's how much he has sent monthly. The girls adapt very well to living with just mommy and Miss Didi, as they call her. For Araba, adjusting to waking up to a structured job has been easy because of her last-minute stint at Scentio after Toju's accident.

The morning that she left with the girls, she had checked into a hotel, but she had gotten a new apartment in Maryland within a week. With basic furniture and lots of love, they settled in nicely. Initially, there was no call from Toju and that alone cemented her resolve that she was doing the right thing at the time. After all, if she truly meant something, he should have called, at the very least.

She had initially planned to withdraw the girls from their school, but when she saw the receipt of their school fees in their bag one day, she realised that Toju meant to keep paying their fees. She decided to allow him to take care of his children. She owed them that much. She beams at her reflection against the mirror on the picture frame. No, she doesn't have to hide behind make-up to feel okay anymore. She is free to be herself.

Her job as an art director doesn't pay enough to maintain her old luxurious lifestyle, but the pay cut is a tiny price to pay for her peace of mind and her health. She doesn't have to keep pretending to anyone anymore.

It wasn't until over a month after her flight with the girls that she got her first call from Toju.

It had been at night, and she was in bed reading after the twins had dozed off. A familiar reggae tune started serenading her auricles. She grinned and started singing along to the lyrics as she located the phone on her dresser, glad for the umpteenth time that Sunny, her colleague, had helped her find a more appropriate reggae ringtone.

Emancipate yourself from modern slavery... None but ourselves can free our minds.

BeGone | Temi Taiwo-Oni

Seeing Toju's name on the screen, she reflexively muted the call and stared at the screen. She was unprepared for the call that night. She looked about her as if a sanctuary or superhero would materialise to shield her from facing him. When the ringtone picked up again, she steeled herself and took a deep breath before picking up the call.

"Hello," she tapped the loudspeaker icon and placed the phone on the pillow beside her.

"Hello, Araba."

Silence.

"Araba, are you there?"
"Yeah... Toju, I'm here."
"How are you?"
"Much better than I have been in forever."
"Hmmm! I guess that's on me. How are the girls doing? Are you all coping well?"
Silence again.

"Araba?"
"Still here, Toju. We are all getting by and getting used to the change."
It was Toju who kept silent then, but Araba did nothing to encourage him.

"I would have called you earlier..."
"Toju, you owe me no explanation. I'm not giving you any."

"Don't worry. I'm not making any demands on you. I just called to let you know that I'm sorry. I'm really, really sorry about all I put you through."

A soft moan escaped from her lips. She wasn't sure if he heard it, but she knew she had to take charge of the call.

"Good night, Toju."

She had clicked the end button and pushed the phone away from her. A split second later, she picked up the phone and put it on silent. She didn't want him calling back, at least not that night. Toju had let her be that night and never called her again at night.

A few days later, she had received a bouquet at her new office. She was so sure that it was an error when she was called to attend to the delivery that she turned the delivery guy back. The note had read, 'Have a great day, Babe!' There was no other message, not even her name.

An obvious mistake. Who is babing me?

The next day, the delivery guy returned with a second note.

For you, Araba the Elegant.

Only one person on the planet had ever called her by that name. She had accepted the flowers. Since then, she had received one bouquet a week, every Monday.

Next, Toju started sending her voice notes. They began with messages for the girls where sometimes he sang or read a story. Other times, they were just messages telling them how he was doing or how his day had gone. For the sake of the girls, she indulged it. She never said a word to him but allowed them to send messages back to him.

Then, about a week ago, he sent a message that was for her. She had listened to it repeatedly and by now, she knew it by heart.

Hi Araba, I'd like to see you, just to talk a little. I've missed you, missed you very much. I know you don't want to talk, or you'd have sent me a message. I may have said a lot to you over the years, and listening to me may be the last thing you want right now, but please... give me a chance to see you and talk to you. After all I did in the past, I know that I don't deserve you, but I hope that you will allow us to start afresh.
I love you, Araba.
Your undeserving husband, Toju.

Her heart had melted on the spot. Emotions that she had long buried and thought were dead, levitated to the fore. She was glad to be alone and sitting in the office when she had listened to the message. It had taken her three days to respond.

Okay.

That was all she had written. His reply came a minute later, and they had arranged a date for the meeting. It would hold tomorrow, Saturday. The girls would be dropped off at Chii's, and then they would meet at a quiet bar in Ikeja. That was the plan. Today, however, she leaves the office on time and picks Sparkle and Rosie for an afternoon of ice cream and waffles, a treat that they have started indulging in at least once in two weeks.

BeGone | Temi Taiwo-Oni

Toju looks up as Joe, his new assistant, opens the door to his office and walks in.
"There you are, Joe. Please, clear up my schedule for the day. I'm going out. I have an appointment I don't want to miss."

"Alright, sir. I just need your signature on these documents, and I'll be out of your hair, sir."

Toju reviews the documents he hands to him and takes his time to sign off.

"Should I ask Onoja to bring your car around now?"

"Yes, please, do that. I'll be out of here in the next twenty minutes. You can pick these up then."

Taking the hint, he quietly exits the office, shutting the door behind him. Joe had come highly recommended by Mr Benton after having Angela transferred to a different department. She was resourceful and though nothing had gone on between them, keeping her on was not worth his marriage. Feedback from Mr Benton proved that she had settled well with the marketing team, so it all worked out well.

BeGone | Temi Taiwo-Oni

He sits back and surveys the wall to the left of his table. His wandering eyes find what they seek, the Forty-inch portrait of Araba he had made after she fled from him.

It was great that he recovered most of his pictures and other media from his cloud accounts. The portrait was based on a photo from their honeymoon, and he'd had it made as a reminder of who he once was and what he had lost as a result of that.

A quote was written underneath the portrait, which was etched in his memory though not legible from his vantage point.

Do not allow your past to prescribe your future, but allow it to enhance part of who you will become.
Anonymous

Oche had stayed on after Araba went away and helped him find a therapist, the same one he has an appointment with today. The two of them had helped him through his physical and emotional recovery from the trauma of the accident and his separation. The letter Araba had left him in her bedroom was devastating, but he had allowed her to have her way. He still has it in his wallet, where he had kept it as a keepsake.

Toju,
By now, you will have noticed that I have left with the children. I can't take the pretence and affront anymore. It's time I move on. You have gravely damaged me, and I have tried to stay on to give you the support you need, despite our history. Your sister hasn't made it that easy, and seeing you today with your assistant; I realise that I no

longer have a place here, and I do not have what it takes to take my pound of flesh back from you as I intended. I ask for only one thing, LET ME GO!

I won't bother you or ask you for money. I got a job today. Someone sent my sketches to an art competition, and I got a call to make an appearance. Today, I have been offered the job, and ~~I think~~... I know that it's what I want to do.

I wish you all the best with Angela & I hope she makes you happy. Araba.

It had taken persistent counselling and encouragement from Oche before he could pick himself up. Aunt Sylvia had ranted and raved about how callous Araba was to have left in such a manner, but he had stormed away each time she raised it. Before long, she knew not to mention her around him. Two days after he was relieved from needing nursing care, he had gotten her a ticket back home, and she hadn't argued with him.

In the days that followed, he visited the twins' school to confirm they were still there, and then he tailed Araba from the school to her office one day. His plan had come together in bits.

Tomorrow, he would be meeting with his Araba, making yet another step closer to recovering his wife and children. His friendship with Oche has blossomed, and he has learnt quite a lot from the young man.

He recollects Oche's statement, "We can all be better than we think we can, but we can't do it all by ourselves. We need people. People need us."

With that thought, he places the letter back in his pocket and tucks it into his breast pocket before picking up his laptop bag and heading out.

The End

Author's Note

It's been a pleasure to share Araba Cole's story with you, and I hope it marks the beginning of a long relationship with my stories.

Already, some have requested for a sequel to this book and I would like to hear from you, your thoughts on this novel and a subsequent sequel. You can share your reviews on any of my social media pages below:

Facebook: https://www.facebook.com/temitaiwooni/

Instagram: https://www.instagram.com/temitaiwooni/

Twitter: https://twitter.com/tywhytoni

To keep abreast of updates on BeGone and other novels from me, follow me on these handles.

Please, leave me a review on amazon as it will really help my growth as an author. I sincerely want to hear whether and how this story resonates with you.

You can also send feedback and comments about the book directly via temitopetaiwo-oni@outlook.com

Thank you once again for reading till the end. I trust it was a refreshing read.

Temi Taiwo-Oni

About the Author

Temi is a Nigerian writer, copywriter and brand strategist born in Kano, Nigeria and she grew up in Lagos.

An alumnus of Eketi Ette's creative writing Workshop, she spent 12 years in banking before transitioning to the world of brands and storytelling. BeGone is her first published work of fiction and her short story, Oblivion is due to feature in the UEA CWS anthology 2022. She currently lives in Norwich, UK.

Printed in Great Britain
by Amazon